DYNAMI

Spur watch
rawhider wo
biggest was
quick killing
He would
escape. Sp
that way.

"You o
the wago
have th

Also in the *Spur* Series:

SPUR #8

SANTA FE FLOOZY

DIRK FLETCHER

LEISURE BOOKS NEW YORK CITY

A LEISURE BOOK®

December 2003

Published by

Dorchester Publishing Co., Inc.
200 Madison Avenue
New York, NY 10016

ISBN 0-8439-2201-X

Visit us on the web at www.dorchesterpub.com.

SPUR #8

SANTA FE FLOOZY

CHAPTER ONE

(The year was 1874. General Ulysses S. Grant was in his seventh year as President. A U.S. baseball team traveled to England for an exhibition game. Goal posts were used in football for the first time that year at Cambridge, Massachusetts. The Greenback political party was organized. The first recorded kidnapping for ransom was staged in Germantown, Pa. King David Kalakaua of Hawaii was the first reigning king to visit the U.S. Barbed wire, the development that would spell the eventual end to the wild west, was invented that year by J. F. Glidden in De Kalb, Illinois. The Cathedral of San Francisco de Assisi was over half completed in Sante Fe, New Mexico in 1874. Work began on it in 1869. Hamilton Fish continued as Secretary of State in the Grant administration.)

SPUR MCCOY lifted the Colt .45 and cocked the six-gun with his right thumb, then edged up to the corner of the adobe block building on a side street in Santa Fe, New Mexico. Sweat furrowed down through dust on his forehead as he tensed against the bricks. With a sudden lunge, he charged around the corner.

Two shots blasted hot lead on him, but already Spur had dived forward into the dust, his .45 spitting flame as fast as he could pull the trigger.

The two men in the alley stared at McCoy for a second, then the first looked at the black hole in his leather vest and brought his hand up to touch his shirt that had blossomed with a red rose before he groaned and slid sideways into the alley. His nose plowed a line through the dust, the soft dirt building up a pile of dirt against his forehead, covering his eyes as the outlaw died.

The second man had no time to wonder. The .45 slug burrowed a straight hole through a rib, then his chest and his heart. It killed him instantly and he slammed backwards from the force of the big .45 lead messenger of death.

Spur McCoy nodded and sat up, then felt a stinging in his left arm. He looked down to find the upper sleeve of his light blue dress shirt stained red with his own blood.

"Damn!" he muttered.

Three men ran into the alley and stared at the dead outlaws. One of them ran back to Main Street.

"He done killed them bank robbers!" the young man screeched. "He gunned 'em down in the alley!"

6

Spur knew the sheriff would come, asking questions. And he would show them his credentials and fill out the necessary papers. But before that he wanted to look at his arm.

Spur holstered the .45 and grabbed his left upper arm with his right hand and winced. Annabelle Dare would look after it for him. She was better than a sawbones any day, and a damn sight prettier. He stood and walked back to Main Street. Half a dozen men hurried past him to look at the dead men. Two women chattered as they tied on sunbonnets and scurried toward the alley.

McCoy was tired. He had been chasing the two bank robbers for almost two weeks, all of it on horseback in the high desert. Now he wanted a hot bath and a bed, and he knew Annabelle could supply all three, including Annabelle herself in the bed. He tried to grin but he was too tired.

Annabelle stood on the porch of the Santa Fe Carriage House looking his way. When she saw him she lifted her long skirts and hurried down the steps to the dusty street. She met him halfway across the avenue which was an inch deep with powdered dust from the continual grinding of steel wagon wheel rims and horses' hooves.

She had never looked prettier. He swore she was no more than five feet tall, with a pile of blonde hair on top of her head to make her look taller. Her face was round and pixie-like, with darting brown eyes, high pink cheeks and a cupid's bow mouth. Now her pretty face wore a

7

frown.

"The idea, Spur McCoy, is to shoot the bad guys without letting them hit you. Gracious! You gone and got yourself wounded again. Don't you ever listen to what I tell you? Menfolk will be the death of me yet. Inside! Inside with you and let me get out my alcohol and scissors and bandages. I swear, Spur McCoy, I just don't know what I'm going to do with you!"

She was beside him then, holding his right arm, and "helping" him forward despite the fact that he was two inches over six feet tall and weighed twice her own ninety-eight pounds.

Spur laughed softly. "I bet you'll think of something to do with me," he said softly so only she could hear. He saw a trace of a blush color her neck and then she lifted her head and turned toward him.

"Yes, of course I can tie up a gunshot wound. I *am* a frontier woman, after all." She said it for the benefit of two ladies walking by. Both were of Mexican ancestry, and were leaders in the Spanish speaking section of town.

Quickly they went up the steps, through the lobby and into the door marked "Manager." As soon as the door closed behind them, Annabelle threw her arms around his neck and pulled his face down so she could kiss him.

When the kiss ended she sighed.

"Damnit, McCoy! You've been in town for two days, and haven't even stopped by to say hello."

"Hello, Annabelle Dare," Spur said and kissed her. He felt her press her delicious body against him and he moaned. "Hey, we have lots of time. First the arm?"

She kissed him again, then kissed his arm.

"Mommie kissed it and made it better."

"Mommie can do even better, though, can't she?"

Annabelle grinned and rolled up his sleeve, but the fabric was too tight.

"Awwwww. Have to take off your shirt," she said.

He unbuttoned the blue shirt and stripped it off. She admired his muscle-sculptured upper body for a moment, then looked at his arm.

"At least the round went on through." She was all business then, filling a pan with water and using a cloth and lye soap. She washed the blood off his arm and from around the wound. It had started to clot. She took a clean square of cloth and pushed it over the back of the wound which was the larger hole.

"Hold that there while I get some whiskey."

"Terrible waste of good booze."

"Hush up. The sheriff will be here soon." She brought a bottle of whiskey from the cabinet and uncorked it, then sloshed some across both wounds.

"Eeeeeeeeeha!" Spur whooped as the alcohol hit raw nerve endings.

"Yeah, if it hurts, it works. Doctors finally found out what we were doing with the whiskey. Now they tell us the alcohol in the whiskey does something good for the wound. We been telling the sawbones that for years."

9

She poured more whiskey into the wounds, then used a clean roll of bandage made from a bed sheet and wrapped up Spur's arm so the clean compresses she had put on both sides of the wound would stay in place. When she came to the end of the bandage she tore the strip down the middle, put one end each way around his arm and tied the ends together with a hard knot.

"You should be a nurse," Spur said.

"I am. Now, the sheriff first, or a bath first?"

"The sheriff, and that bottle of rotgut." He took the whiskey bottle and tipped it up, gulped down a couple of swallows and lowered the fire-water. He drank two more shots of the whiskey, put the cork back in and set the bottle on the desk.

"Now, let's go find the sheriff."

The lawman was coming into the hotel when they walked out of the office. It took only a few minutes. The other men had fired first, according to witnesses, so it was self defense. Period, end of report.

Spur relaxed. He would not have to prove who he was. Lately he had found things worked out much better for him if no one knew his official capacity until they had to. It made his job easier all the way around. Now he shook hands with the sheriff, and followed a small Mexican boy who said Spur's bath was ready.

When Spur got to the bathroom at the end of the hall on the second floor, he found a steaming tub of water. It was one of the new long tubs you could sit down in and stretch out your legs.

Beside it were two pails filled with cold water. On a chair were two large, fluffy towels, a bar of lye soap, and on another chair, his saddle bags and the carpet bag from his mount.

Spur dug into his pocket, found a liberty seated quarter and tossed it to the boy. The young Mexican-American's eyes widened.

"Gracias, senor!" he said and hurried out. It was probably more hard money than he had seen in weeks. A grown man worked all day to earn a dollar these days.

McCoy locked the door after the boy left and stripped, then he heard a noise behind him. A door at the far side of the small bathroom opened and Annabelle stepped in. She wore a white robe and carried a bath brush.

"I heard, sir, that you wanted someone to scrub your back," she said and smiled.

Spur stood there naked yet totally at ease, and stared at her. "Only if you'll have a bath with me," he said.

She let the robe fall open and then pushed it off her shoulders so it slid to the floor. She was all white and pink naked flesh under it and a swatch of soft blonde crotch hair.

"I *love* to take baths. And if you hadn't asked me, I was going to volunteer." She walked toward him, swaying her hips, her small round pink-tipped breasts thrust forward, bouncing and jiggling with her movements.

Spur caught her shoulders, then bent and kissed each blooming breast, making her suck in a breath of surprise and appreciation.

"How long has it been, beautiful-man Spur?"

"I was here about a year ago."

"And then I was in St. Louis and missed you at Christmas."

"We'll make this our Christmas," Spur said and kissed her lips gently. Her mouth was open and her tongue darting at his closed lips until he opened them. He pushed her away a minute later and tested the water.

Boiling. He added a bucket of the cold water. Still too hot. After the second bucket of cold water he stepped in, and held out his hand to her.

"I remember we got into all sorts of contortions the last time we tried this," she said.

"First, we wash off my two week's worth of trail grime, then we think about weird positions."

She nodded, grabbed the soap, brush and a washcloth, sat down in the water and began washing his back. He told her what he had been doing since he had seen her, and she said not much had been happening in Santa Fe until now.

When the washing was over, she turned and leaned her back against his chest and drew his hands in front of her to hold her breasts.

"That's nice," she said.

He petted her breasts and kissed her neck. "It gets better."

"I've heard it can't be done underwater."

"Have you tried?" he asked.

"No."

"How about now?"

"Anything," she said.

12

Spur had her move forward, then he soaped his erect phallus thoroughly and, staying out of the water, eased her back to him. Still facing her away, he lowered her slowly and his sabre slid easily into her ready scabbard.

"Oh, my God!" Annabelle yelped. "You did it!"

Spur eased back into the water and they both giggled. A minute later they had sloshed a bucketful of water out of the tub.

"So that's why they say you can't do it in the tub!" Annabelle said. She eased away from his hard shaft, then stood and stepped from the tub, holding out a towel. Spur dried her, taking pains that her breasts and crotch received special attention. She motioned him into the next room and he found it to be a second bedroom joined to her suite below by a spiral staircase. The bed was the largest he had ever seen.

Annabelle turned back, put her arms around him and held Spur tightly.

"Hold me close," she whispered. His arms came around her and she pushed against him.

"Spur McCoy, I'm feeling shy. I . . . I don't want you to think I'm a loose woman. I mean, I don't jump into bed with every man I see. You're a special person, do you know that? I tried to trick you into marrying me once, re- member? The trick almost worked, but you said no. I know you're not going to marry me, but I can still dream. And now, right now, Spur, I want to dream again. I want to pretend that this is my wedding night. Would you let me do that?

13

The ceremony is all over and we're home and you have just undressed me and now I hope that I can please you so you'll take me to bed."

He could feel the heat of her loins soaking into him. Her breath was hot on his chest as he tilted her head to kiss her. Annabelle's breasts were twin cones of fire burning into his chest.

Their lips met.

Never had he felt lips so alive, so burning with anticipation and desire. He kissed her again, then nibbled at her lips as she moaned in joyful expectation. He felt her hips pressing against him. Then they began a soft movement that soon turned into a slow grinding against him. She parted her legs and moved slightly so his leg came between hers, and the soft hair caressed him. Then he felt the thatch parting and a soft wetness pressing hard on his leg. One of her hands slid between them and grasped his turgid shaft.

She moaned again, and chewed at his lips, then moved her mouth lower and licked his nipples. Her breath came quickly now and her eyes closed as she sucked.

Spur bent and picked her up. He reached down and kissed both her breasts and she climaxed in his arms. Her small body shook, jolted, and trembled and she gasped for breath as the spasms rolled through her again and again.

He lay her on the bed and she caught his shoulders and pulled him down on top of her. Again the tremors flashed through her and he saw that her legs were spread and her pubis thrusting upward against his legs.

"Now, darling! Now, please now! Come inside me and make the whole world perfect!"

A moment later they had joined and her arms were around him, her legs locked over his back and she purred throatily like a tigress as tears slid down her cheeks.

"I always cry when I'm the most happy," she said, then closed her eyes and thrust against him as Spur lay there suspended over her, barely touching her small form.

"Lie down on me hard, with all your weight," Annabelle said. "It feels good when you're crushing me."

Slowly they both built to a gentle, soft kind of lovemaking that Spur found most rewarding. It built and built until she gave a soft cry and her whole body spasmed under him, triggering his own response and they both cried out softly and moaned and panted for breath as the physical release came and he settled down gently against her again.

"Oh, yes!" she said, holding him tightly with her hands locked around his back. "I'm never going to let you get away from me again!"

Spur was still sucking in air from wherever he could find it to replenish his drained system. His breath came like a volcano for another two or three minutes before he could begin to think straight.

He eased most of his weight to one side on a pillow and she nodded a quick thanks.

It was ten minutes before either of them moved again, or said a word. Then she looked at him.

"I hope you won't be leaving, now that you caught the bank robbers."

"I'm a working man, Annabelle li'l darling. I go where the boss sends me."

"Uh-huh. But the boss doesn't have to know you're done. Don't you deserve a few days vacation? When did you have your last little bit of time off?"

"Don't remember."

"Then stay a few days. I can't promise it will always be as sweet as it was this time. Lordy! But you do get me wound up tight! I just want to stay in bed all day and all night with you!"

"It was great."

"Then stay a while."

"We'll see. Depends how good the cook is here at your hotel. I've been eating trail food for almost two weeks."

She pushed him to one side and sat up, her breasts bouncing. He captured one with his hand.

"Anything you want to eat tonight! You just name it and we'll kill the goose or go find the fish or hunt a pheasant! Anything you want! I mean it. Give me an order right now so I can go get our cook started!" Her eyes were flashing, darting brown beacons. Her face was so alive and vivacious he was amazed. She was a remarkable little lady.

"Ready? You have a pencil and paper? You won't be able to remember all of this." Spur waited until she had the paper, then he began reeling off exactly what he wanted to eat for supper.

....

.

CHAPTER TWO

THE MAN WHO called himself Zack White sent a
stream of brown tobacco juice past the ponderosa pine he lay behind and stared more
intently at a small ranch just below in the
valley. He was only fifty yards from the cabin,
but he saw no one moving. Zack rested easily,
chewing on the wad in his mouth, and then spitting at insects that crawled on the high pine
country forest floor. He had time. Nothing else
to do but sit and wait. They would come out
sooner or later.

It was an hour later, almost noontime, when
the cabin door opened and a teenage girl walked
out carrying a bucket. She took it to the well
pump twenty yards from the house. The girl had
pretty, ripe-wheat-straw blonde hair and good
tits. Zack rubbed his fly and grinned.

"Keep yer damn shirt on, big stick," Zack said
staring down at the bulge in his dirt-stiffened

18

brown pants. Things were starting to move; it would happen soon.

A woman with the same color hair and not much over thirty came out and stared at the girl who hurried her pumping and lugged the heavy pail of water back to the cabin.

Ten minutes later a man rode into the clearing on a plow horse, dismounted and tied the heavy animal to a post. Then he pulled off his shirt and scrubbed his hands, face and torso at an outdoor washstand.

Zack put his hands to his mouth and made the call of a hoot owl. Hoot owls never out this time of day, and if they were, they wouldn't advertise it by calling. He gave the call a second time and with it came the sharp report of a rifle from across the clearing.

The rancher below spun around, a Spencer .56 caliber slug through his shoulder.

Zack pulled his six-gun and ran down the slope screaming at the top of his voice. He heard his two sons, Birch and Piney, screaming the same way. The boys got to the wounded man first and were about to put a knife into his throat when Zack stopped them.

"Boys, ain't I never done taught you no manners? Feller here ain't harmed us one little satchel full. I reckon his missus can patch up his shoulder. Fetch her and the girl, too."

Piney nodded and ran for the cabin door.

A shotgun boomed into the mountain stillness outside Santa Fe, and the three men dove behind any cover they could find. The two boys thundered pistol rounds into the one window, then Zack bent low and raced for the side of the cabin. The rancher packed no gun, Zack had made sure of that before he left. He slammed against the log wall and edged around so he could kick the door open. As he did, a blast of buckshot lanced out the opening.

When the thundering roar of the ten gauge scattergun faded, Zack listened intently.

A woman cried softly.

A younger voice whined in protest.

They didn't know how to load the shotgun. He risked a look around the doorframe, and saw both women at a table trying to open the double-barreled weapon.

Zack jumped through the door and, holding his pistol ready, walked toward the women.

The older one was pretty, softly blonde, not weathered and wrinkled yet by the tough, harsh pioneer life. She looked up with deep blue eyes that showed anger and fear.

"Please, don't hurt us!" she said.

"Now why would I hurt you folks?" Zack asked. "Just move away from the shotgun."

They did and he walked toward them. The girl was a beauty, maybe seventeen, better tits than he'd guessed. He stopped in front of the women and reached out. The older woman was shivering, but she held still when he touched her chin.

"Pretty lady," Zack said. He moved on to the girl. Her face turned when he tried to touch her chin. Angrily his hand caught the neckline of her calico dress and he jerked downward, hard. The seams held for a moment, pulling her head lower, then the threads broke and her dress and chemise ripped to her waist. Both breasts swung into view and Zack grinned.

"Nice tits, little filly. Knew you had good ones." His hand fondled them, and the girl turned her head away and burst into tears. The woman leaped at him, clawing at his face. Zack backhanded her with his closed fist. The blow caught her on the side of the face, scraped off skin and drove her to the hard packed earth floor.

"No reason to get hurt. Just do what we say, and don't go clawing us. Understand?"

The old woman nodded. The girl would not look at him.

A moment later he caught each woman by a hand and pulled them out the door. They stumbled after him, the girl trying to keep herself covered. Zack led them to the washstand and dropped their hands.

"My turn first, Paw, you promised!" It was the wheedling voice of his youngest, Piney. The young man's long fingers stroked the fly of his britches. He was shorter than his brother, and his shoulders were narrower, but he was the best man with horses Zack had ever seen.

"Well, hail, Piney. Why not? We get to watch. How about over there in that patch of shady grass under that golden cottonwood?"

Piney already had his pants open. He yelped in delight, sprang forward and grabbed the girl by both hands and tossed her over his shoulder. The girl screamed in terror.

"No! By God, no! Leave my little girl be!"

The roar of fury came from Willard Bukowski as he surged to a sitting position, holding his bleeding shoulder.

Zackery White sent a squirt of tobacco juice at Bukowski, then kicked him in the face with his heavy boot, dislocating his jaw, tearing his nose half off and gashing a three-inch wound in the thin flesh over his eye. Bukowski dropped to the ground and lay there.

"Asshole! You keep quiet or you're dead in five seconds. Savvy?" Zack's eyes narrowed, his face worked with sudden hatred.

Bukowski lay in the dust and weeds. His eyes couldn't focus yet, but he looked where the voice seemed to be coming from and nodded. Mrs. Bukowski whimpered as she saw the man wearing grease-stiffened, filthy clothes drop her daughter to the ground and kneel beside her.

"Sir! Have mercy on my daughter. She knows . . . she knows nothing about men."

"Shit! And her that big? Reckon she's gonna find out damn quick. You want to get closer to watch?"

Murial Bukowski turned away and stared at the house.

"Tie him," Zack said to Birch. Zack's oldest son was twenty-three, and his father figured he was slow witted. But Birch jumped to the task with rawhide strips he drew from his pocket. He tied Bukowski's hands behind his back, then reached for the man's ankles.

Bukowski slammed one boot into Birch's

stomach before the younger man fell on his legs and tied his ankles.

"Now look at that!" Zack said.

Piney had stripped down the girl's dress and was licking and sucking on her breasts. The girl was on her knees, her hands tied behind her back. She was not trying to get away.

Zack turned to the woman. "Your turn," he said.

She watched him. A long sigh came from her and her shoulders sagged.

"If . . . If I let you do . . . do what you . . . you want to do, then will you leave us alone and move on down the trail?"

"Fucking right! Won't hurt you none at all. Girl over there will be smarter, and you can patch up your gun-shot husband."

Zack reached for her breasts. She pulled back.

"Don't play games, bitch!"

"How . . . how do I know you'll keep your word?"

"Trust me."

Bukowski roared in protest where he lay near the washstand. Birch dumped the washpan full of water over his head and cackled with laughter.

Slowly the woman began to unbutton the front of her dress. Zack's rough hands pushed hers away and he ripped the front of the dress apart, popping buttons and tearing the fabric. A chemise covered her breasts.

"Soak some," Zack said to Birch. The oldest

son grinned and grabbed a bucket of water.

"Take the rest of them off," Zack said to the blonde woman.

The girl under the tree screamed. Zack saw Piney holding her down on her back. He lay between her spread, kicking, creamy white legs, as he jammed his hips at her crotch.

"Dear God, tell him to be gentle with Cynthia!" Mrs. Bukowski wailed.

"Him? You worry about me, cunt!" He tore the dress off her, then the chemise. Zack grinned at the size of her breasts, full and with heavy brown circles and thick, thumb-sized nipples already rising.

He pulled down her cotton petticoats and looked with delight at her lush V of blond crotch hair. Zack grabbed her by one breast and pulled her forward until they were four feet from her husband, then pushed her down on the dirt.

"Makes it better when your man over there can watch. Bet he's never seen anybody else fuck you."

Murial screamed and tried to crawl away. He hit her in the face and she screeched in pain, but fell on her back. He spread her legs and unbuttoned his fly, spit on his hand and coated his penis before he jammed it into her vagina hard and fast, searing the unlubricated flesh, bringing a howl of pain from both the woman and her husband.

"Bastard!" Willard Bukowski screamed. But then he could scream no more as Birch tied wet rawhide around his throat. It was tight enough so talking was uncomfortable. The sun gleamed down with noontime heat on the scene, and even as Bukowski thought about it, the wet rawhide began to dry and shrink back to its former size before it had been wet and stretched.

"Now, Paw?" Birch asked, a whine in his voice.

"Christ, go ahead."

Zack looked away. He had always known something was strange about his firstborn, but he had never expected this.

Birch used his sharp knife, cut the front of the pants off Bukowski until his genitals were exposed, then gently, lovingly, Birch began arousing the furious man who lay bound, and half throttled by the rawhide.

Zack was nearing his own satisfaction. He always liked women with big tits and a tight cunt. He gave one final series of long, hard thrusts and grunted with his climax, then rested on her soft body.

Birch was busy behind him. Zack usually never watched, but this time he turned just as the rancher's extended phallus vanished into Birch's mouth.

Under the golden cottonwood tree, Piney had finished the first time and was playing with the pretty girl's young, soft body. Zack could hear him talking to her, promising that he would be careful and gentle if she helped. Soon Piney was after her again.

Zack heard the horse coming and didn't look up. He knew the sound—it was Zelda's nag. The horse stopped and a scream of delight and madness greeted him as he looked up.

"Jesus, husband! Don't you know how to control your issue!"

Zelda slid down from the horse, pulled off the doeskin squaw dress she wore and ran to Bukowski. She backhanded Birch along the side of the head, spinning him away from the prostrate, excited man on the ground. Zelda looked at Bukowski a minute, then squatted over him, lifted his still turgid tool and lowered herself on it. As it slid into her vagina she squealed in delight and moved back and forth gently. She talked quietly to Bukowski all the time. A minute later she rested some of her weight on her hands and began riding his phallus like she was a jockey at a horse race. She grinned at Zack and every thirty seconds let out a scream of lustful satisfaction.

Zack looked back at the woman under him. Her face had been turned away. He was excited again. He came out of her and pushed upward until he sat on her cushiony breasts and thrust his erection at her mouth. Her eyes flared and she screamed at him.

Zack knew she never would take him in her mouth, and his big hands slapped her twice. Then his fingers closed around her throat and he lay on top of her again as his fingers tightened more and more. Her eyes were wide, then rolled upward until only the whites showed. They came back and she tried to scream but couldn't. Her fists beat on him but the force became less and less until at last her hands fell to her sides. He held tightly until the

26

last shiver and twitch had left her body. Then he stood, buttoned up his pants and went into the house.

The fun was over. Now it was time to go to work. A family like this would have cash money hidden here somewhere, all he had to do was find it. Zack began by tearing the cupboard apart, then he systematically destroyed the inside of the house.

Outside under the tree, Piney talked soothingly to the girl. She told him her name was Cynthia.

"You liked it, didn't you, the fucking?"

Cynthia was still crying. She blinked. "Some of it was good, but it hurt so. Does it always hurt?"

"Next time will be better."

"I couldn't!"

"You can if I say so," Birch thundered, saying it just the way his pa would.

She let him play with her breasts. There was nothing else she could do. His knees held down her hands by her sides and he sat on her stomach. His . . . his . . . *thing* hung there limp and shrunken. It was ugly, horrible! She rose up a little and looked at the well where she saw her mother lying naked on the ground. Oh, no!

"I want to get up now," she said.

"Well, ain't that dandy. I want to fuck you again."

"No."

He slapped her hard.

"Woman, you do what I tell you to do!" For a moment he was furious. He wanted to hit her

27

again and again. Then he took a breath and he got control again. His anger cooled, and he smiled. "You sure as hell are pretty, and you got beautiful, big tits. You want to come travel with us, be my woman?"

"No, I can't leave my parents."

"Hell, you'll change your mind."

"*No!*"

He reached for his pistol and put the muzzle in her mouth. "I say you come, little pussy, you come or I blow your brains out. You understand?"

Eyes wide, terror in complete control of her now, she nodded. He took the gun away.

"You want to come away with me? I'll be good to you. We got money, plenty to eat. Clothes even, you want. We get lots of clothes. You come with me?"

"Yes," she said softly.

Piney brightened. "Good, let's go tell Ma. You can do the cookin' and dishes and keep the fire. Ma will like that."

He stood and lifted her up.

"But I don't have on my clothes."

"Don't matter, Ma probably don't neither by now." He laughed and his voice went high and wild.

He took her hand, pushed his privates back in his pants and buttoned them, then led her toward the well.

They were twenty feet away when Piney looked up and saw Birch glaring at him. Birch pulled up his big handgun and fired three times. All three slugs hit Cynthia in the chest. She was dead before her body slammed backwards three feet to the ground.

Piney stared at his brother, then at Cynthia. He knew she was dead. He charged ahead, jammed into Birch and knocked him to the ground.

"Why the hell you do that? Why you kill her? She was coming with us!"

"Sure, and you get all the fun. Pa said no, last time. Right, Pa?"

Zack had just come out of the cabin. He knew what had happened the minute he heard the pistol shots. A look at the girl confirmed it.

"Done is done. Don't do no good to jawbone 'bout it now. We travel light, you done been told, Piney. Now, help me, you two. We got work to do. Piney, run fetch the wagon. Somebody might stop by. We got to move smart."

The three White men looted the Bukowski cabin of everything of any value that could be sold. As they worked, Zelda White sat beside Willard Bukowski. The sun was rapidly shrinking the rawhide now. It cinched tighter and tighter around his throat. Only a wheezing gasp could bring air into his lungs now.

Zelda sat in the dust, rocking gently back and forth as she watched the man beside her. She knew he was dying. It was simply part of the ritual. She was not going to let him die alone. She rocked and sang a little lullaby. She used a different one each time. The tune went on and Bukowski gasped and wheezed as his eyes pleaded with her to cut the thongs.

Zelda shook her head. He should know that

she couldn't do that. It wasn't fair, there were rules that had to be obeyed. Besides, Zack would slit her throat if she even tried to save one. He had been good, though, long and thick, best she could remember in the past six months. Zelda sighed. His hands were still behind him, but his arms were twitching, then his legs jerked and for a moment she thought he was dead.

A rasping, keening kind of sound came from deep in his throat, then his eyes stared at her without moving. She saw a jet of urine stain the pantsleg that had been cut away. She made the sign of the cross over him, stood and walked toward the house.

Zelda wondered if this lonely cabin would have anything that would sell in Santa Fe.

A half hour later the covered wagon was loaded with everything of value in the house. The two horses in the corral had been tied behind the wagon and the one cow had been slaughtered and half the carcass tied to the side of the wagon. They would eat well tonight and for two days until the meat spoiled.

Zack headed the wagon down the faint trail toward Santa Fe, still two days' drive away. He would meet with his two brothers before they came to the New Mexico Territorial capital. Zack wondered how his medicine man brother and the outlandish fake itinerant preacher were doing. It was a kind of contest, to see who could steal the most between the larger towns where they would arrange to meet, stay a few days and enjoy the fruits of their hard work.

Zack slapped the reins on the two sturdy mules. The blonde rancher woman had been good. Someday he would push Zelda over a cliff and claim himself a younger wife. Someday soon. He turned to look at Zelda who leaned on a pillow against the side of the wagon and slept. She was snoring and her mouth was open.

Zack nodded. Someday soon, bye, bye Zelda.

CHAPTER THREE

SPUR MCCOY LINKED Annabelle Dare's arm
through his as they strolled down the boardwalk in Santa Fe's more "proper" district. That
was the stretch from the Santa Fe Carriage
House to the McGill Drygoods Emporium, a
distance of more than fifty yards with some
twelve to fourteen retail establishments in-
volved. Along this respectable area of old Santa
Fe, there was not a bawdy house, bar nor
gambling den.

"Mr. McCoy, it's been a delightful evening. I
especially enjoyed the roast quail and dove
under glass, then the wine and now a walk in
the twilight. How romantic!"

Spur held her arm tighter. He could learn to
get used to talk like that, and a woman like this,
and a town like Santa Fe. What was he
thinking? Even if the "quail" and "dove" were
chicken, it had been a delightful meal.

"Miss Dare." He stopped. She looked at him

out the corner of her eye and he began again.

"*Mrs.* Dare. Respected hotel owner and widow of the late and lameted Douglas Dare. It has been an honor and a privilege . . ." He stopped and they both broke up laughing.

She tugged at his arm and he felt a small lift as she pulled him firmly and intentionally against her breast.

"McCoy, you've simply got to stay for a week at least. There must be something else around here that needs to be checked out by a federal lawman . . . The post office! Yes, that's it! Our mail delivery is terrible. Do an investigation for me about the post office. That should take you at least a week!"

He held her arm tighter and angled across the street toward a medicine wagon that had lanterns out. Someone had let down the side of the wagon which formed a platform where the medicine hawker evidently gave his pitch. There were half a dozen men and women standing there waiting for the show to start.

"Now here is something I could investigate," Spur said.

Annabelle laughed. "Silly. You know these medicine shows are harmless. So they sell a little colored water mixed with fifty percent whiskey. Who knows, maybe it will cure everything from rheumatism to old age."

"Maybe it will," Spur said. "I've also heard of some of these guys who sell worthless railroad stock on the side, and seduce young girls under the guise of treating them. Why do you suppose they move around so much?"

"Get run out of town?"

"At least half of them. Most sheriffs watch the roving medicine man like he had the plague."

"Then you don't have to."

A trumpet fanfare blasted into the gathering dusk, and a man wearing a flowing black robe and a top hat pranced onto the small platform. To him it was a stage. He had a dramatic flair that caused Spur to frown.

"Ladies and gentlemen of Santa Fe! Greetings. I come to you all the way from Boston, in the great commonwealth of Massachusetts, far across this great country of ours on the Atlantic Ocean. I bring you some of the latest in medical discoveries, some suggestions how you can live a happy and a longer life, and I have a few surprises for you along the way.

"For instance, do you know that sometimes when you get sick it's because of little bugs that are so small the human eye can't see them except through a magnifying microscope? A Frenchman is starting to call them bacteria. And bacteria probably cause almost all of our diseases. When we figure out how to control and kill these bacteria, we'll put an end to sickness and perhaps even death itself!

"And now for another amazing product—Dr. White's fantastic Lifeline Tonic, absolutely guaranteed to perk you up, to help with rheumatism, neurology of the extremities, the common cold, and those strange women's ailments that come every so often. This amazing elixir is scientifically blended and balanced by some of the top medical experts in their respect-

34

ive fields, and combined into a practical and inexpensive home remedy that today is used by millions of good Americans just like you."

"Hey, Doc. How much it cost?" a man's voice asked from the rear.

"That's the good doctor's shill," Spur whispered to Annabelle. "He buys a bottle and gets things moving."

"My good man, this elixir is not for sale. No, not at any price. However I have been franchised to make it available to you on a long term lease arrangement, at one dollar a bottle. Only one dollar for more than a pint of this magical medicine that has had the blessing of the thousands it has cured, from the Atlantic coast all the way to California."

"I'll take a bottle," Spur said, holding up a greenback one dollar bill. He moved to the front of the wagon.

"Sir, would you happen to have a gold piece?" Doc White asked.

"Afraid not, Doc. Isn't a greenback good enough for you?"

"It's better than a Continental! Certainly a greenback is fine with me, sir, and here is your bottle. Tell your friends. Now, ladies and gentlemen, I am sorry that I have only a limited supply. However I have a few bottles left, and will be more than happy to return here tomorrow night with a fresh supply straight from Boston. Now who will be next?"

Spur and Annabelle moved down the block, then turned and walked back past the wagon. As they crossed the street again, Spur saw a small boy slip into the back of the medicine wagon. A moment later a second boy, about twelve, went under the dark canvas and into the wagon.

Spur shrugged. No reason the fast talking medicine man couldn't have a family with him, which could include two boys. Spur tightened his grip on the lovely Annabelle and marched back toward the hotel.

"I have some paintings in my downstairs living room I want to show you," Annabelle said smiling seductively.

"And some etchings in your bedroom?" Spur asked.

"One or two, if you insist on looking."

Behind them, Dr. Rusty White found his crowd was fading quickly. A down-and-outer probably without a nickel to his name was the last one standing near the wagon.

"My good sir, I'm sorry but the last bottle of Dr. White's amazing Lifeline Tonic has been snapped up by a thankful public. However, if you'll come back tomorrow night . . ."

The bleary-eyed man shook his head. "Hell, I ain't buying none of that stuff. Got a bottle in Cheyenne once, same poison. Almost killed me."

"Get out of here, you miserable drunk, before I call the sheriff!" White snapped.

The drunk held up both hands, shook his head and wandered down the darkening street.

Dr. White closed up his wagon and stepped inside. He looked at the four young boys in front of him and smiled. Santa Fe might turn out to be a good place to do business after all. He motioned for Luke and the thirteen-year-old jumped up and stepped to the front of the wagon.

"Now, what have we here, only three?" White whispered.

Luke bobbed his head. "Honest, I looked hard all afternoon and three was all I could find. I had to give them each a quarter to get them to come."

"They know what they are to do?"

"Sure. I told them, convinced them they could make more money than they ever seed."

"Good." He turned to the boys. "Have you had supper, yet?"

All three shook their heads.

"Well, we can't have that, can we? Luke, go to the cafe across the street and bring back eight big sandwiches and a gallon of milk. That should fill up your bellies." He gave Luke a greenback and the boy scooted from the wagon.

Dr. White turned to the boys, his expression grim.

"Young men, don't think that you are getting a free supper, or that you won't have to earn the quarters you already have. You'll earn it all. First some questions. From what Luke says, none of you have mothers or fathers who will be worried about you, correct?"

Two nodded. The third scowled.

"My paw went on a trip and I been staying with some friends. But they don't worry I'm gone a few days."

"Good. Now, how old are you lads?"

Two were ten, one was eleven.

"And you're good at climbing trees and buildings, I'm told."

They all nodded.

"You'll have supper, and then a nap. Later tonight, I'll wake you for your final instructions. You all know what you're going to do?"

One boy shook his head.

"Luke should have told you. I'm going to train you to be the best little thieves in the world. And you are going to eat better than you ever have before. You will be shown certain houses and you will slip in and steal any valuables you can find. We want jewelry, money, stocks and bonds. Nothing else. You'll be aimed at the best houses in town which have no live in servants. Nobody locks their doors in Santa Fe, so it will be easy."

By midnight the boys had eaten their supper and had had four hours sleep. White roused them and told them again exactly what to do, where to look for valuables in the houses and how to get away if they were discovered.

"Remember, you will go in, take the money and jewels and come back to the alley behind the church. Do *not* come back to the wagon. If any of you are caught, you do not know me. Tell them you were just playing a trick on the owners. If you say I sent you, I will find you, and cut off both your feet! Do you understand me?"

Dr. White had raised his voice to a shrill

shout, and the boys all jumped in surprise and alarm. The medicine man recovered his composure.

"But I'm sure you won't have any trouble. You'll work in teams, and each of you have four houses to search."

He gave them each a sack two foot square with a shoulder strap that went over the head and under one arm. It gave them a place to put the loot and leave their hands free.

"Now, off you go, and good hunting!"

Dr. White sat back in his chair in the wagon, lit a cigar and poured himself a glass of brandy. He had been in town two days and had selected the houses carefully. There would be only two nights to work the houses; then word would spread and the population would hide their money and valuables better and in the well-off owner's houses, they would leave a servant up all night.

Tonight the targets included the territorial governor's house, that of a judge, and several wealthy merchants. All he needed was to hit a big haul in one house, and the whole operation would be dramatically profitable.

He wondered how his brother Zack and Erick were doing. Rusty had no idea what last names they were using now. They changed theirs about as often as he did his. With any kind of luck he would win the contest again. He snorted. How much money would you expect to raise by selling household goods stolen from some poor dirt farmer or rancher? And a preacher took months to set up his flock to be plucked clean. Yes, he was the best of the three operations. He had told them that a year ago.

And there were always the side benefits. He thought of Luke. He was so young and pure and unspoiled. Absently, Rusty White let his hand reach for his crotch and rubbed. They should be back by about four in the morning. If the boys did well, they would have a real celebration!

Luke walked down the dark alley with his partner, Rufus.

"Nothing to be afraid of. We go in the houses, and most of the people leave money laying around. We just pick it up, look in all the places I told you to look for money and jewelry and walk out of the house. We got to be quiet, and if anyone wakes up, we stay still and hide until they go back to sleep."

"I'm still scared," Rufus said. "Never done this before."

"I have—fifty, sixty houses. It's easy." Luke paused and looked across at the first house. It belonged to the territorial governor, and held the best chances. "Come on, this is it. We'll go down the alley and in the back door."

It was a warm July night. Doors of many of the houses they had passed had been left open to catch the cooling breezes. They found the back door of the governor's house and crept up three steps of the porch. No lights were on inside. Luke tried the screen door. It was held by a hook. He took out his knife and pushed it through the crack between the door and jamb and lifted off the hook.

Inside, they went up the open staircase to a long hall. Four doors stood open. The first room was empty. In the second one a young girl slept. She wore only a thin nightgown and it had been pulled down to reveal one pink breast. Luke looked at her for several seconds, then went to the next room.

A woman slept on her side beneath a light blanket. Luke saw a necklace lying on a dresser. He put it in his sack. A jewel box with two drawers sat beside it. He pushed the whole box into his sack and went through a reticule next to it. In the coin purse he found ten double gold eagles and a wad of paper money. He took the coin purse and then silently opened the dresser drawers. In one, under some women's clothes, he found a flat box. Inside was a strand of pearls. He took them from the box and dropped them into his shoulder sack.

Rufus had stood at the door, watching, listening. Nothing moved in the house.

They crept to the next room, where they saw the governor laying naked on top of the sheets. His wallet and gold watch lay on a night stand beside the bed. Rufus picked them up and lowered them into his sack. Then he and Luke looked in two drawers.

The governor suddenly sat up in bed.

"I won't sign the damn bills!" he said loudly. Both boys froze where they were. The governor coughed, lay down and continued sleeping. They found nothing more.

Quietly then went down the steps and out the back door. A block down the dark alley, Luke stopped, opened the jewelry box and dumped everything in it into his sack, then pushed the box itself deep inside a garbage can that still glowed with the remnants of a fire. The small box would be burned to ashes before morning.

Luke did not stop to look over their loot. He put the contents of Rufus's bag into his own and they went on to the next house on their list.

By three A.M. Luke and Rufus were back at the alley meeting place. In a sheltered spot between two buildings, Rusty White examined the take in the light of a small lantern he had brought from the wagon. He smiled as he opened the governor's wallet. Inside were more than two hundred dollars in paper money, as well as a snap pocket with four double eagles. The jewelry from the governor's mansion alone had been a bonanza. He was sure of four diamond rings, and the necklace had three diamonds in it as well as two rubies! The other team had found much less, but they had the secondary houses. When it was all put together, Rusty White figured his small friends had produced over a thousand dollars' worth of goods, including over four hundred in cash!

He gave each of the three boys three greenback dollar bills and showed them where they could sleep the rest of the night. He warned them again sternly about not telling anyone what they had done.

"Lads, if you so much as sneeze about this, I'll cut off your feet sure as I'm standing here. We work together, we keep our mouths shut, and we all make money. Now off with you."

Luke and Rusty walked back to the closed, dark medicine wagon where it sat just off the main street near the edge of town. They stepped into the wagon and Rusty lit a lamp.

"I'm tired," Luke said.

"Yes, so am I. We'll help each other go to sleep." Rusty was a slender, tall man, with a clean shaven face and straight black hair. He stripped out of his clothes and sat naked on the edge of the bed built into the side of the wagon.

Then he undressed Luke, who was four and a half feet tall and starkly white under his clothes.

"I'm real tired," Luke said.

"I know, I know, and we'll sleep. But first we have to celebrate. You did fine tonight, Luke." Rusty kissed his cheek, then lightly kissed Luke's lips and pulled him into the bed on the soft quilts. Slowly the man's hands began to caress the boy.

"I know you're tired, Luke, but I want to show you how much I appreciate your help. Then both of us will go to sleep just real easy."

Luke swallowed hard and tried to relax.

The man's hand drifted down to Luke's crotch and played with his genitals. Luke gritted his teeth, but he couldn't stop his penis from reacting, enlarging.

Rusty moaned softly and Luke rubbed wetness from his eyes. He had to remember to relax . . .

CHAPTER FOUR

ANNABELLE'S PRIVATE SUITE at the Santa Fe
Carriage House was delightful. She had ripped
out a few walls, had some new ones built and
turned four hotel rooms into a comfortable,
impressively decorated apartment. She and
Spur sat on an antique love seat she said had
come across on an early English colonist ship.
Annabelle wore a thin silk gown that hid
absolutely none of her charms.

The bed was mussed from recent use and now
both sipped at a wine she said came from
California, a smooth port.

"I don't know enough about you, Spur
McCoy. I know that you are a United States
Secret Service Agent, and you keep that a secret
most of the time. Your office is in St. Louis, and
you do a lost of traveling with the whole West as
your responsibility. But that's about all I know.
You blow into and out of my life like a New
Mexican tornado."

She reached over and kissed him, then turned and leaned against his bare chest and brought his arms around her. "Now, while we're resting up, tell me your entire life's story."

"It's boring as hell."

"That's for me to decide."

Spur sighed. He wasn't close to many people, especially during the last few years with this wild West assignment. He sipped the wine, let his hand curl around Annabelle's delightful right breast, and began.

"What I didn't tell you before is that I grew up in New York City where my father was a merchant. I graduated from Harvard in 1858 and worked in some of my father's firms for two years. For the next couple of years I was in the army making it to Captain in the infantry before an old family friend called me out of the army to Washington, D.C. He could do that—he was a United States Senator, and he wanted me as his aide. Had enough?"

She shook her head and brought his other hand around to cover her left breast.

"So when the U.S. Secret Service Act was passed in 1865 I applied and was accepted. I took some training and then went to work. We were the only federal law enforcement agency at the time. Nobody else had jurisdiction across state or territorial lines, so we did a lot of work on wide-ranging problems. They set up our group originally with the sole task of preventing currency counterfeiting."

Spur reached down and kissed her neck and Annabelle purred. "Then what happened?" she asked.

"I had served six months in the main office in Washington, D.C. when they decided they needed a man out West. That meant everything west of the Mississippi. Since I had won the service marksmanship contest and was the best rider in the bunch, they sent me to St. Louis to open an office. And here I am."

She turned around and kissed him.

"You forgot the important stuff. You're six-feet two and must weigh about two hundred pounds. You're about thirty-two years old now and your hair is a little on the brownish-red side, and I *love* your thick moustache."

"You have any other complaints?" he asked.

"Yes, you're naughty, just *naughty* in bed!"

"Only twice, so far today." He stood and reached for his shirt. "The sheriff is due back in town. I need to talk to him."

"Now?"

"Right now. He went on a ride north to meet some of his men he sent out this morning to check on a ranch fire somebody thought must be a log house burned out back in the hills."

"Damn." She pouted.

"And I'll be back as soon as I get a couple of things straightened out with the lawman."

"Does he know who you are?"

"Not yet."

He pulled on his boots and tucked in his shirt, then bent and kissed her softly on the lips.

"You stay put until I get back." He touched her breasts through the filmy material. "I wouldn't want you to catch a chest cold in that thing."

Five minutes later, Spur sat in a chair across from Sheriff George James.

"Rawhiders, Sheriff? You sure?"

Sheriff James was a small man, who wore a black suit and a white shirt and black string tie, because his wife thought he should. He stood barely five feet four inches, but he ran a tight and honest political organization that was the envy of the rest of the state. Now he slicked back his thinning black hair and preened a heavy moustache.

"Had all the signs. Family of three wiped out, women raped, one strangled, the young one shot. Both naked. The livestock run off, a cow slaughtered and half taken away, five or six horses trailed behind the wagon. The cabin had been looted and then burned to the ground. Same for the barns. Nothing left."

"Indians, maybe?"

"No. Not from what my men report. The clincher was the way the man died. Had wet rawhide wrapped tight around his throat, then they let it dry in the hot sun. The poor bastard slowly strangled to death as that stretched rawhide shrank."

"Now that sounds familiar to me. We had some reports six, eight months ago about a gang of rawhiders in Oklahoma and Texas. Always killed at least one in the family with rawhide around the throat. The name White mean anything, Sheriff?"

"Seen some posters on them. The White Brothers. I seem to remember there were two of them."

"Three. And all about as dirty and treacherous killers as you'll ever meet. But their real name isn't White—it's Schmidke. A woman in the bunch seemed to be the worst."

"You think we got the White brothers—I mean, the Schmidke brothers around here?"

"Might even be in town already."

"We have over five thousand people here. I can't know all of them."

"They will be trying to sell the goods they stole. You can have your men watch for that. Especially selling off a wagon. I take it your men lost the tracks of the rawhiders?"

"Dozens of tracks, leading off in twenty directions. I've heard of false trails, but my men said they had never seen so many. I only sent two deputies, and they had to give up when it got dark."

Spur reset his low-crowned brown hat on his head. "Now that is sounding more and more like the Schmidke brothers."

The sheriff looked up. "Mister, you said your name was McCoy, but nothing else. You some kind of U.S. Marshal or something?"

Spur took out a wallet he carried, pried apart two tintype pictures and took out a thin printed card. It carried President Grant's signature and proved that he was a U.S. Secret Service Agent. It asked local authorities to give him cooperation in anything he asked.

"Right, figures. I heard about you guys once. Not many of you out here in the West. What can I do for you?"

"You know I came to town hunting those bank robbers. But that case is closed now. I was getting ready to head out of town, but with a trail of the Schmidke brothers, I think I better stick around for a while."

"Want to look at the massacre site?"

"Seen enough, Sheriff. I hear the group splits up and goes separate ways, then comes together in some town to live it up. Wonder if Santa Fe is the site of their next meeting?"

"You have descriptions on them, McCoy?"

"Not much. Just ages, as I remember. Look through your wanteds, we might get lucky. As I recall they are from thirty-six to about forty-five. Only one of them was married."

"Sounds damn near impossible to find them."

Spur stood and grinned. "Yeah, and I like impossible. Let me help you with those wanted posters."

They looked through the posters for almost an hour and at last found what they were looking for. The brothers were wanted for twelve murders in Kansas, six in Colorado, and fourteen in Texas.

"And that wanted is most a year old," the sheriff said.

"I just got my next assignment. Changed my mind about going out to that burned-out ranch. Tell me how to get there. I want to light out first thing in the morning."

The sheriff drew Spur a rough màp. The place

was about eighteen miles out and a thousand feet higher than the elevation of Santa Fe, which sat in a valley at 7,000 feet.

Sheriff James shook his head and watched Spur. "Hell, McCoy. How we going to find these yahoos once they get into town? The wanted says they usually clean up and act halfway civilized while they're in town. How the hell we gonna spot them?"

"Maybe watch for some strangers spending lots of money," Spur said.

The older man laughed. "McCoy, this is special session time for the new legislature. Half the folks in town are strangers, and most of them are spending the taxpayer's money. We got to do better than that."

"True, most true. That's why I'm riding forty miles tomorrow so I can try to find some little clue we can use against them."

"Good luck. I'll tell the livery man to put your mount on my bill. You will want a fresh horse?"

Spur said that would be fine and made a round of the saloons. He lost track after the first dozen. Nowhere did he find an example of a rawhider with grease and dirt stiffened clothes, unkempt beards and long hair, coupled with a nasty disposition.

Back at the hotel, he used the key Annabelle had given him and found her waiting for him, wearing the same transparent gown and reading a book. She put the book down and came to meet him.

"Where's the bed?" he asked.

"I like a man who's direct."

He told her he had to be in the saddle at four A.M. For a moment she pouted, then he told her he would be staying in town on another case, and she kissed him.

"Marvelous! Then I'll let you go to bed and sleep tonight. But tomorrow night I have a surprise for you."

"I'm not sure there are any surprises left," Spur said.

Annabelle laughed. "There are quite a few, and this one you're going to love!"

Spur barely got undressed down to his briefs before he fell into bed and went to sleep at once.

Annabelle sighed, kissed him on the cheek and cuddled close against his back. Then she slept too. It was good to have a man in her bed again.

By daylight, Spur had ridden up more than five hundred feet and could see Santa Fe far below in the valley. He was working into the Sangre de Cristos mountains, and could see several snow-capped peaks. He was on a trail of sorts. It headed almost due east toward the settlement of Las Vegas, and then on into Texas.

He left the trail and turned north at a lightning shattered pine tree. The jagged stump still stood eighty feet high and served as a landmark for travelers. He found the small stream he was to follow and let his mare drink. Then he pushed on. He figured it would take him five hours to find the ranch. The uphill climb was taking a toll on the mare and he rested her frequently.

Two and a half hours after sunrise, Spur found the ruins of the ranchita. The three fresh graves had not been molested. He found blood on the ground and was glad he had not witnessed the slaughter.

For half an hour he scoured the remains of the house and barn. Nothing. The rawhiders knew their work well. He drank from the stream, ate a pair of sandwiches he had talked the hotel into fixing for him, and then began to circle to find the wagon tracks. The tracks led in three directions, and despite attempts to cover the wheel marks, he found where two of the trails wound back over rocky stretches and came to the ranch again. One set of wheel prints did not backtrack.

He followed that one for a mile, then found a jumble of new wagon and horse tracks. In the army, Spur had worked through dozens of puzzles like this one. The winner was the one with the most patience. After an hour of tracking and backtracking and marking trails he had followed, he came to the one true track that led away from the mess, and angled downhill toward Santa Fe. He circled, found two tracks that later melted into one and then got down from his horse at a sandy area near a stream and studied the wagon wheel prints and those of the horses.

At once he decided the wagon pullers were mules. They seemed to be heavy and short gaited. There was nothing distinctive about their hooves, and only one was shod.

The wagon wheels were easier to read. An old Johnson freight wagon, if he figured it correctly. More than likely with bows and a cover on it to hide the stolen property and give some privacy. The front wheels on a Johnson were offset six inches inside of the rear wheels. No one had ever told him why, but it made the wagon easy to track and pick out of a crowd. Most freight wagons had axles the same width, and their steel-rimmed, wooden-spoked wheels tracked one on top of the other.

Twice he found where the wagon had to backtrack to find a safe route down the mountain; then it hit a gentle valley and a stream that paved the way toward the city below.

Spur left the tracking then, picked the quickest route and rode for town. He was looking for a Johnson freight wagon, maybe with bowed, covered top and loaded to the sideboards with stolen household goods. Should be simple.

He tried to remember where he had seen such a wagon before. Before he got to town he thought of one. The medicine man used a Johnson, a big heavy duty rig, and it had built-on sides and a top. But the medicine man's rig had been parked on the street three days before the sheriff said the attack on the ranch took place.

Clear one Johnson wagon owner of suspicion.

Spur came into town trail-weary just before dusk. He had been in the saddle for sixteen hours. He was hot, bone weary, and so hungry he could eat a side of raw beef.

Annabelle delighted in playing nurse and hostess. She fixed his bath and ordered dinner for him and picked at her food as she watched him. Spur almost went to sleep as he ate fresh strawberries and cream for dessert. He got through the cherry tarts and then staggered to the bedroom.

Annabelle whooped in delight as she jumped on the bed beside him, only to find Spur McCoy already sleeping, one arm thrown over his face, and his other hand resting on his genitals.

She sighed as she pulled off his boots and then his pants and spread a sheet over him.

Tomorrow night, she thought as she lay down beside him. It was nice just having him there. Tomorrow night for sure they would make wild, passionate love.

She gazed at his relaxed face for a moment, then reached over and kissed his cheek. She had a problem. How was she going to convince Spur McCoy he should quit the Secret Service and settle down here in Santa Fe with her? The hotel made plenty of money, and he could manage it if he wanted to. Or he could raise a few cattle on a little ranch she owned outside of town. It was a problem, but one she was going to enjoy working on!

CHAPTER FIVE

"OH, YES! SISTERS and brothers in Christ, I say Amen. Amen to the love of our heavenly father!"

"Amen!" someone in the small group gathered outside the covered wagon said. The side of the wagon held a small platform with a pulpit on it, and behind it stood a man of thirty-six, dressed all in black, with a beneficent smile on his face.

It was just dusk in Santa Fe, and Spur McCoy had passed the preacher as he rode in from the massacre site. Lanterns were hung ready to light when it grew dark.

"My sisters and brothers in Christ, the theme for my talk tonight is love. The good book is full of love. No man hath greater love . . . Love thy father and thy mother. Love God. I say unto you, love one another. God loves a cheerful giver."

Eric Thompson checked his gathering as he spoke. He had arrived in town three days before and put up broadsides on as many buildings as he could advertising the rally and revival tonight. Maybe twenty people out there. Ten who might give. Damn, but this was a hard way to make a living! If there wasn't a wealthy widow in this town who had a soft spot for itinerant preachers, he just might have to go back to more direct ways of becoming rich.

He droned on, describing the delights of the "place my father prepares for me, my house of many mansions." The preaching was no problem—he could do that in his sleep. He could be a spellbinder, but how could you wring gold pieces out of empty wallets? Mostly he drew lower class worshippers, and they were nearly as broke as he was. Just one youngish widow lady who was a staunch believer, was that too much to ask?

"And so, my new friends, tonight you have seen just a brief glimpse of the glory of Jesus Christ. Just a hint of the marvels that wait for you on the other side. But can we sit and hope for that day? Never!

"Never! We must work here and now for the glory of the Lord! Amen to that! We must improve our lives, be more loving and charitable. We must do the work of the Lord. And how better to do that than to support worthy projects with our prayers, our works and our gifts?

"Brothers and sisters, I am a humble servant of the Lord. But even I and my horses must eat a crust of bread or a fork full of hay. I have taken a vow of poverty, and all of your gifts and offerings go directly, I say *directly*, to the work of the Lord. Praise his name!"

"Amen!" A big husky man standing near the platform said.

Erick took two offering plates from the pulpit and handed them to the big man.

"Brother, would you be so kind as to pass these among the fine folks here and allow them to contribute to the Lord's work? I thank you, Brother. I thank you for the Lord, through our spokesman and our saviour, Christ Jesus."

There was a rustle of clothing as reticules were opened, as wallets and purses came out of pockets. He reached for a glass of water and drank slowly, watching the flock. It was so new to them, this first day. He needed time. In time he could extract plenty from them, perhaps even make a living. But it was that one big mark he was searching for.

His gaze traveled over the group, now numbering about twenty-five, he figured. Average. No one dressed well. His eyes held on a woman near the far side. She was better dressed than the others. She stood tall and straight, and while perhaps forty still had a remarkable figure. She was watching him, and he nodded to her, then looked on. The plate came to her and she emptied a handful of coins in the plate. He prayed they were double eagles!

A moment later the burly man returned the two plates to Erick which he held high.

"O, Lord of all men! Oh, Jesus Christ our

Savior! We do thank thee for these offerings, bless those who gave of their treasure, bless them in every way. We dedicate this bit of thy abundance to the work of bringing Jesus to every man, woman and child in Santa Fe! In Jesus's name we pay . . . Amen."

Erick held the plates high a moment more. A dozen "Amens" came from the audience. Then he put the plates onto the shelf in the small pulpit. With one hand he collected the bills and coins and pushed then into his pocket out of sight of the congregation. Before he ended his next few sentences he had emptied the plates. Yes, he felt gold coins!

"My new friends in Christ, I thank you for coming. If any among you need spiritual aid or counseling, my door is always open. Think of this as a rolling church wagon, dedicated to Christ and his way of life. And remember, do unto others as you would have them do unto you. We will have another meeting here tomorrow afternoon, and again in the evening. I pray that all of you can return and bring two or three families with you. This is a family Christian Revival, and I pray I will see you again. If any of you have burdens you wish to let me help you with, please come to the front immediately after the service. Now for the closing benediction. Would you all please bow your heads in prayer.

"May the Lord bless you and keep you, may the Lord make his face to shine upon you and be gracious unto you. May the Lord lift up his countenance upon you and give you peace. Amen."

Erick stood as the flock slowly moved away from the wagon. One young man held back, then changed his mind and walked away. To Erick's surprise the nicely dressed woman he had noticed before stood beside the back of his wagon, waiting. He stepped to the ground and walked to her.

"Pastor Thompson," she began, then hesitated. "I . . . I don't know how to say this."

He could see her plainly now. She had a handsome, somewhat stern face, high cheekbones that lent a note of arrogance to her features, and deep blue eyes that told of many mysteries. Most of her soft brown hair was covered by a small hat.

"Please, do you wish to step inside? Others might be curious."

"Yes, of course."

He preceded her, going up the three steps to the back of the wagon, lifting the canvas door so she could step inside.

She looked around, saw the lit lantern and nodded.

"Oh, my, it is so homey, almost like a living room. I've never been inside a covered wagon before."

"Thank you, ma'am. It is my living room, and my kitchen, and where I retire as well. Do you wish to sit down?"

He pointed to a rocking chair with a soft cushion he had won from his brother in a poker game. It was a beautifully carved chair. She murmured something and sat, knees together, on the edge of the seat. Now she turned her concerned eyes toward him.

"Pastor, I'm not catholic as most of Santa Fe is because of its Spanish origins. There's no Protestant church here and I feel left out. This is the first real service I've been to in almost a year. I'm deeply indebted to you for your kindness."

"My great joy in serving the Lord is seeing how quietly and gloriously he works in mysterious ways. Perhaps there is some higher plan that directed my path here tonight." He let her think about that for a moment, then he went on.

"I'm sorry I don't know your name."

"Oh, how stupid of me. I'm Hillery Gregson, Mrs. Hillery Gregson. I'm pleased to meet you." She held out her hand and Erick held it, then bent and kissed it.

"Always a pleasure to meet a beautiful woman, especially when she is so dedicated and consecrated to our Lord Jesus Christ."

"I was hoping I could talk to you about staying on in Santa Fe. I would be more than willing to help a fund-raising campaign to build a Protestant church. I'm not sure which persuasion you are. My own background is Methodist."

"Well, Sister Gregson, I am honored and flattered. Up to now I have refused all such offers, but I truly like this town. I think we could find enough dedicated Protestants here to form a church, and I will certainly consider the matter carefully. Since I have taken a vow to poverty, there is little I could contribute, except my enthusiasm, my calling to be a preacher, and my dedication. I'm not an old man yet—I think it would be a great challenge to build a church here. But I will think more, and of course, the most important part—I will pray about it."

Hillary Gregson smiled. "I am so pleased, Pastor Thompson. I'll do some more thinking about it too. I did some planning a year ago concerning a church. I'll find those notes and think it through again. I am so thrilled that you're considering it!"

Her face lit up as she talked and she became almost pretty.

She watched him closely for a moment. "Yes, yes, Pastor Thompson. I think you're exactly the man we need to start our church." She went to the door, then turned. "Would you consider coming to my house tomorrow night so we could discuss the project with some others in town who are also interested?"

"I think that would be a fine idea, ma'am."

"Good! I'll be at both your services, then drive you to my home in my carriage. Until tomorrow."

He helped her down the steps and walked with her to her buggy just down the street. A sleeping driver came awake and helped her into the rig, then wheeled it away down the street.

Erick Thompson grinned broadly as he

returned to his wagon. He had a fat fish on his line! Now all he had to do was play her carefully. His retirement from the "ministry" might be just around the corner! Quickly he took down the lanterns, closed up the pulpit and platform, and stepped into his wagon.

A girl sat on the bed built onto the front of the rig. She definitely was not Mrs. Gregson. The dress she wore left her shoulders bare, her lips and cheeks were red and pink, her hair piled high on her head, and the top of the dress had been pulled down so it came across her breasts just below large brown nipples.

"You! I told you not until the service was over!" Thompson hissed at her in a stage whisper. "You trying to ruin me?"

"The fucking service *was* over, and I got a good look at Mrs. Gregson, the rich bitch. Not much of a looker, but she's really got a yen for you, I can tell. You can flip up her dress any time you want to, Pastor, and bite her pussy."

Quickly Thompson snapped the canvas door shut and put two security boards across the back of the soft canvas of the wagon. Then he advanced on the girl who now pulled her skirt up so he could see a swatch of black crotch hair.

He sat beside her and fondled her breasts. "June, you are a total whore. But the next time you get here so early, you get half the pay. And if you breathe one word about me to anyone . . . you hear, to *anyone*, I'll slice your pretty tits off and let you bleed to death. Is that clear? Can that pea-sized brain of yours understand that?"

"Yeah, yeah." She caught his hand and

pushed it between her legs. "Talk about pussy, it's more fun!"

She pulled his head down to her breasts and his mouth covered one of her delightful mounds.

Pastor Erick Thompson sighed. "Glorious! Now get that dress off. You've got a mountain sized heat built up in me. And that Hillery Gregson! She would be something to upset in a bed, just to see what it did to that smug expression."

"I tell you, you can get her into bed anytime you try. Still, a couple of weeks of warmup never hurts with a frozen biddy like her. Now, let's talk about me. What are you going to do to me tonight that is delightful? You can't fuck me any way you did last night."

Erick let her undress him, turned down the lamp so their shadows wouldn't show on the canvas, then slapped her round bottom until it turned red and she moaned with rapture. He pulled her up on her hands and knees and she giggled, pushing her bottom at him.

"Oh, God! I like it this way. Which hole?"

"Both of them, you silly little whore. First one and then the other all night long until I've fucked your brains out."

"Cost you ten dollars."

"All night is *five*, you fucking whore!" He lunged forward, penetrating and driving in until his pelvic bones hit the soft cushions of her buttocks. He moaned in pure animal pleasure and pumped into her fast. Then he slowed. There was no rush, he had all night to introduce this little slut into the marvels of being a temple whore. It didn't really matter what the temple was, or who it was dedicated to, just so the little priestess was willing and able. This one was both.

Erick smiled. All this fucking and a rich widow on the line to boot! It was a fine day! He was sure she was a widow. He would find out first thing in the morning. Either way, he was determined to bed her and rob her, one way or the other.

CHAPTER SIX

IT HAD TO be a dream. The giant grizzly bear licked his face again, but the beast's breath was sweet. Spur tried to get away but he was trapped under a heavy log. The bear moved to Spur's ear and repeated the licking and Spur began to giggle and laugh and try to get the grizzly bear to stop tickling him that way.

Something soft and scented touched his face and then his face and he knew it couldn't be the grizzly. He tried to roll over, to get rid of the dream, but something held him pinned to the rough forest floor.

The eight foot tall grizzly roared, but the sound came out as a tinkling bell-like laugh.

"You must be awake now," a feminine voice said.

Spur started to answer but when his mouth opened, something soft and sweet smelling surged into it and he sputtered and his eyes snapped open.

No grizzly bear.

No log pinning him down.

Rather a naked Annabelle lay on top of him on the big bed, and one of her generous breasts dangled half in his mouth. He grinned, moaned in contentment and chewed on the delicate mammery morsel.

"I think you finally woke up," she said. "I wanted to seduce you in your sleep, but you didn't cooperate."

She moved her other breast into his mouth as he began to talk.

"Even things up or she'll be jealous."

Spur chewed on the other breast for a minute, then eased away from her, rolled her to one side and sat up beside her.

"I hear some people think it's evil and wicked to make love in the morning," Annabelle asked. "Do you?"

Before he could answer she kissed him. He caught her and rolled her on her back, spread her legs and eased down on top of her.

"I think it's monstrous and pagan, especially if it happens to me when I'm sleeping so I can't enjoy it."

"You are a little crazy, but I love you all the more for it." She watched him closely as she said the words, but he didn't react. At least he didn't yell and scream at her.

"Aren't you supposed to be getting me all sexy feeling?" she asked.

"It's your party. I thought you were seducing *me*."

Annabelle frowned. "Did I tell you about my

husband, Donald? He was twenty-one years older than me. And he died. His heart gave out, and I never told anybody, but we were making love that night when it happened. He just yelled and grabbed his chest and fell on top of me. Talk about dead weight!"

"Now this is erotic talk. I'm really getting excited," said Spur dryly.

"Naturally I didn't tell anybody. You know what the gossip would have been in this town? So I just didn't tell a soul. I got dressed and put Donald under the covers and ran for old Doc Cunningham. I wanted you to know."

"Thanks."

"Kiss me, McCoy."

"No more story of your life?"

"No."

Spur kissed her and worked his tongue into her mouth, and soon he felt her temperature rising. Her hand wriggled between them to his crotch and found what she was seeking. Her breath came quickly and he moved his mouth to pink flowering buds on her breasts. Her slender body writhed under him.

"Lordy, that feels wonderful!" she said.

His hand moved up between her quivering flanks and caressed the soft pubic hair.

"Now, darling. Please right now! Come inside me, quickly!"

They joined smoothly, perfectly and for long moments Annabelle couldn't speak. She brimmed with surges of delicious feelings that left her shaken and spent, and fulfilled all at the same time.

Later they lay in each other's arms.

"Darling, I wish it could be this way forever. Not just once a year, but every morning of the year. Wouldn't that be heaven?"

"I'd be used up by the time I was forty!"

"You would not! Donald used to say, 'use it so you don't lose it.' "

"And look what happened to Donald!"

"Don't remind me!"

He slid away from her. "I am supposed to be working. A quick breakfast in the dining room while you get the rest of your beauty sleep, and I'll see you later."

Spur dressed in some old jeans and a blue shirt.

"They don't match your brown eyes," Annabelle said drowsily.

Spur threw a pillow at her and let himself out the door.

All morning he worked the trail he figured the wagon would take into town. It was the closest to the mountain where the bushwackings took place. Then he figured what he would do if he were in the Schmidke brothers' place: he'd go around and hit the town from the other side. He had saddled up his horse for the search, and now rode to the far side of the small town and began questioning people in the houses closest to what he figured would be the rawhider's route.

At the fourth house, an old man came to the door. He said he had seen the prairie schooner sail in day before yesterday, but he wasn't sure where it landed.

"One of them big wagons with bows and a canvas cover. Looked loaded down heavy. Pair of mules had all they could do to drag her along. I used to have one like that back in sixty-two."

Spur thanked the old man and moved on. Two houses later, a woman said her little boy had called her out to take a look at the wagon. There weren't many like it around in that area. She knew that it had gone down a ways, then turned left, toward the outskirts of town again. Spur thanked her and moved on.

He stopped his horse where the woman figured the rig had turned left and looked. There were ten or twelve houses out there, half of them with barns and outbuildings that could hide a wagon. That's what Spur would do with the rig if he wanted to come in town and not be noticed—put the rig undercover and rent or take over a house for a while.

They were here, somewhere. Spur could feel it. He knew they were in Santa Fe. Now all he had to do was flush them out. It would be the older of the trio, with his family. Nobody knew what they looked like. He had to find them, with the wagon. He would do some after-dark scouting and see what he could find. He didn't want to scare them off, not now that he was this close.

But even if he did spot the older brother, how would he recognize the other two in the family who some said were just as bad, but operated in different ways from their brother? It was all one big poker game and he was drawing to an inside straight flush, a sucker draw no matter what the size of the pot.

Spur rode back downtown and checked out the twelve biggest bars and gambling halls. The sheriff was in one of them, but Spur passed him by without a flicker of recognition. He had a beer and made it last. He could find nobody who looked like a rawhider.

He was in the tenth bar in his quest when he stumbled into the middle of a gunfight. It was a Texas Tenderfoot Can't Miss challenge.

The two men stood five feet apart. There was no way either man could miss the other. The first one who could draw, cock the hammer and fire would live.

Spur wished the sheriff was there. Nobody was trying to stop the slaughter. There was no cause for a killing like this.

McCoy walked into the bar and cut lose with a rebel yell he had heard so often for those bloody six months he had been on line fighting the Rebs. Every man in the place looked away from the duelists and watched him. He had out his .45 Colt and kept walking toward the two in the center of the big room.

"It's over, men," Spur said. "I don't know what the argument is, but this is no way to settle it. Both of you take your six-guns out by thumb and finger and lay them gently on the floor."

"No way, Mister," the younger of the men said. Spur guessed he was maybe twenty-one. "He called me names and I don't take that off nobody!"

"Instead of being called a name, you'd rather be dead?" Spur asked.

"What if we don't shuck our guns?" asked the other one, who was probably a year or two older.

"You stand there that way another fifteen seconds and I put a .45 slug in one kneecap for both of you. Neither one of you will ever walk normal again. You want that?"

"What cause you got, Mister? Do I know you?"

"Not up to now."

"Then back off and mind your own business!"

"You got five seconds left."

The older one took his weapon out. The younger one did too, holding it by thumb and finger on the handle. A moment later the guns were on the floor and a man wearing an apron around his stomach ran up and grabbed the irons.

With the excitement over, the rest of the bar patrons went back to their gambling and drinking. The two fighters followed the barkeep, asking when they could have their guns back. He said when they were ready to leave. The two turned and with a death-anger in their eyes looked around for the man who had broken up their party, but Spur had left the bar as soon as the guns hit the floor. He wasn't interested in their problem, or their anger.

At the next bar Spur found a likely candidate. The man was in his forties. The pants and shirt he wore were so dirt stained and stiffened they looked like they would stand up by themselves. The man was wearing a misshappen, dirty hat, and had an unkempt beard that was half gray, half black, and all tobacco stained. He growled and glarerd at everyone who came near him.

Spur asked the barkeep about the man.

"You mean Old Ned," the apron said. "Never have known his last name. He's kind of the town character. He goes from bar to bar and gets two free beers a day just to be himself. Seems like he musta been around Santa Fe since it was founded back in 1610."

Spur thanked the barkeep, then glanced up. "Did you say this town was started in sixteen hundred and ten?"

"True. It was part of the Spanish colony over here, this was the province of New Mexico and Santa Fe was its capital. Only they called it *La Villa Real de la Santa Fe de San Francisco de Assisi*, whatever all that means. They sent in mule trains every three years from Mexico City with supplies."

"Two hundred and sixty four years ago!" Spur said with surprise. "I thought the only thing out here then was pine trees and sagebrush."

Spur thanked the barkeep and moved down where he could watch the customers. He couldn't find a good prospect. The wagon was his only good lead so far, and he couldn't find that, either.

He checked with the sheriff, but the lawman had found nothing to indicate the Schmidke brothers were in town, though there had been a

72

rash of burglaries—four houses broken into last night and money and jewelry stolen.

"Doesn't sound like the Schmidke brothers' style," Spur said. "Never have heard of them being cat burglars. Still, you never can tell. Let's see what happens tonight." Spur didn't tell the sheriff about the Johnson wagon clue. He would wait and see what he discovered.

Spur found a hardware store and bought a box of rounds for his .45 Colt and went back to the hotel. He had to come up with a new angle.

Rusty White sat on the edge of the bed and watched Luke eating the rest of the meal he had brought in from the restaurant. Rusty felt a strange attachment to the boy. He felt like a father to him as well as like a lover. It was all mixed up. He had never let this happen before and he knew why. Luke had been with him now for over six months. There was a real and deep sense of attachment. The others had been quick relationships, spur of the moment things, but with Luke it had been much more.

"Good meal?" Rusty asked.

Luke nodded. "Yep." He looked up. "I got to thinking. I take all the chances, you keep all the money."

"We've talked about that, Luke. I give you ten dollars for every good night we have. You must have over a hundred by now stashed away in your saving place."

"Yeah, but we bring back a thousand, and I get ten. That's not fair."

Rusty sighed. "Didn't I pick you up in

73

Cheyenne just a jump ahead of the sheriff? Didn't I lie for you and hide you when we left town? Luke, ain't I been good to you? You got money, and a safe place to live, and I'll teach you the patter and the trade of being a medicine man, if you want."

Luke pushed the tin plate away and stood up.

Rusty realized the boy was growing up. He was a good three inches taller now than when he had first been rescued. And he was starting to look at women. Maybe Rusty should take him over to one of the fancy lady houses. No, not yet.

"Luke, let's have a little nap and talk about this. I bet we can work it out."

Luke stood where he was and stared down at Rusty White. "First, I want to know how much we took in last night, cash and jewelry. You said over a thousand. How much?"

"Well, I didn't figure it out for sure, maybe fifteen hundred or so."

"Fine. I want half! From now on, I take all the risk, we pay the boys ten dollars each and I get half!"

"Luke, that's crazy! What would you do with that much money?"

"What do you do with it?"

"Luke, let's talk about it. Come over here."

"No. I ain't gonna let you mess around with my privates no more. It's wicked."

"Luke, you better think over carefully what you're saying. You could be out on your ear, sitting on the street, asking strangers for a nickel."

The young man stood taller, then reached down and rubbed Rusty's crotch. "No, you won't do that. You like the way I let you asshole me. You love it! You're a damn queer, and you're trying to make me into one. But you won't throw me out. You like to suck on my prick too much!"

"Luke, I'll give you more money, a hundred dollars every night that you work the houses! A hundred! But let's not rule out being—good friends. I need you, Luke!"

The young boy grinned. "Damn right you need me. Make it two hundred a working night, and we'll leave the rest of it the way it is, agreed?"

Rusty White scowled. The boy had him in a bind. Just then he felt Luke unbuttoning his fly and the young hands crept inside his pants and did wonderful things. Rusty moaned and jerked down his pants, turned on his back and pulled Luke's face over his crotch. He gasped in pleasure as the boy's mouth closed around his erection.

Luke did what the older man wanted him to. He tolerated it, but all the while he was working out a plan of his own. He had seen last night where Rusty kept his money and the jewels he hadn't sold. There had to be five or six thousand dollars there in cash! And enough diamonds to set Luke up in business somewhere.

No more would he have to put up with the vile, ugly things that Rusty did to him, and demanded that Luke do for Rusty. At last he would be free! He would be out from under this weird man, and he would have enough money to last him a lifetime.

Luke knew that he might have to kill the man to get away. That didn't bother Luke. He was practical. His knife had drawn blood before when he was trapped and hungry. It could kill again. Tonight would be a good time, after they got back from the midnight burglaries. Yes, tonight! Then he would be free, and he would be rich!

CHAPTER SEVEN

THE PALE HALF moon disappeared behind a cloud and Spur ran quickly from the side of the house to the small barn behind it. This was his first real chance to find the covered wagon he figured the rawhiders used. The other house and barn had been too close to the street, and the barn not constructed correctly. This one had a large door in the center for a drive-through, probably with cribs and bins inside on the ground floor.

The tall Secret Service agent moved like a shadow to the back of the barn and went through the regular door built into the larger one. Inside it was darker than outside. He pulled a stinker match out of his pocket and scratched it on the rough wood of the barn door.

The match flared into light and the sulphur odor was unmistakable. That's why they called them stinkers, Spur decided.

Holding the match high, he looked as far into the gloom as he could see.

Nothing.

He walked forward slowly so the match wouldn't blow out. It began to burn down and he lit another from it and reached the front side of the barn. No wagon.

"Who the hell's that down there?" An angry voice sounded from above in the darkness.

Spur extinguished the match and crept silently toward the rear door in the darkness.

He heard cursing from above, and the unmistakable sound of a six-gun's hammer cocking.

The shot boomed in the dark stillness. Spur bolted for the back door, sliding through it just as a second shot blasted and a bullet lug dug into the wood beside the door. Then he was outside and running toward the next barn two hundred yards south. The moon had double-crossed him and was shining brightly again. He tried to forget the target he made as he ran.

But no more shots followed him. He got to an outhouse and leaned against it, panting. There was no pursuit. Maybe he had disturbed a hired hand who was sleeping in the haymow.

Spur shrugged and looked at the next barn. Not so promising. A square box with a lean-to on one side. Lamps glowed in the house which was only twenty rods from the house. He moved cautiously, found a rear door on the barn and slid inside. His eyes were more used to the faint light now and he moved slowly, but saw that there was no room here for a big wagon. He went out the back door and tried the lean-to. A canvas draped the front of the opening. He pushed it aside.

A Johnson covered wagon. The tongue had been removed and stored under the rig. He froze, listening. Nothing moved. He slipped under the canvas and looked at the inside of the structure. It was tightly built and would let no light show through.

His match flared and he looked in the front of the rig. It was a rolling home, and stuffed with household goods. It even had the smell of a rawhider's outfit. He blew out the match as he heard the screen door of the house slam shut. Spur crawled under the wagon and waited. Chances were someone was only paying a call on the outhouse. Then he saw the glow of a lantern under the canvas as it was flapped back.

". . . Come get her own damn stuff after this," a voice grumbled. The lantern vanished as the man climbed into the wagon. A moment later the figure jumped down, mumbling to himself and he and the lantern moved away in the night. When the screen door slammed again, Spur came out of the lean-to, and walked quickly toward the next house to the right of this one.

He knocked on the small frame home's front door. It was early and there were still lamps lit in the residence.

A man opened the door cautiously.

"Yep?"

"Good evening, sir. Sorry to be calling so late, but I'm a special deputy for Sheriff James. I need to ask you some questions."

"Never seen you before," the man said.

"I'm new in town. Do you know the people who live next door?"

"Yep."

"Have you seen them in the past two or three days?"

The man frowned. "Can't say as I have. Not hide nor hair of them, come to think of it."

"Who lives there?"

"Older gentleman and his wife. Both must be about sixty. He's got a bad limp." The man looked up quickly. "Something happen to them?"

"I hope not. Did you see a covered wagon rig around here in the last two or three days?"

"Sure did. About dusk one day, came right past the house."

"Notice where it went?"

"Nope."

"What are the people's names next door?"

"Galloway, Frank and Betty."

"Thank you." He started to turn. "Oh, it might be best if you don't go calling at the Galloway's for a spell. There is a chance that something has happened to them, and there may be dangerous people living there now. Just go on as you usually do."

"Outlaws?"

"Could be. But you shouldn't be in any danger unless you go over there."

The man nodded. "Damn! I should have kept better track of the Galloways."

"No fault of yours, sir. Thank you."

Spur left the house and walked back to his horse. There were lights showing through half the windows in the Galloway house. He wanted to kick open the door and start blasting them straight into hell. He would have, a couple of years ago. But now he had grown more cautious, and he played it more by regulations. As far as evidence went, he had none. There was no way yet that he could connect the owners of the Johnson covered wagon with the killings of the family on the mountain.

But he would find some. And he would find out what had happened to the Galloways. He had a strong feeling that the Galloways were both dead. Someone had ridden into town, scouted out the best barn and the best family to take over. Then they did it quietly and came in as close to dark as they could. The Galloways by now were probably in shallow graves behind the barn.

Spur rode to talk to the sheriff. The two lawmen agreed: there was nothing they could do right then.

"We could ride up with a posse and scare the hell out of them and chances are they would panic and start shooting," the sheriff said.

"And the town would lose three or four good men. No, Sheriff. There has to be a better way. I think tomorrow I'll go out there in my best shirt and tie and be a traveling salesman with a fine display of hunting and throwing knives."

"I'll be right behind you."

"No, Sheriff. I have to do this alone. They see anybody else, I'm dead where I stand. I know these kind of people—they kill first and ask questions later."

"In the morning?"

"Soon as I can get some good knives in a kit and ready to go. Maybe about ten. I'll let you know what happens. Any more burglaries reported tonight?"

"Not yet. I got two extra men out walking the better neighborhoods."

The lawmen said goodbye and parted. Spur headed for the Carriage House and that surprise Annabelle had promised him.

It was just after one in the morning when the four boys came back to the alley where they met Rusty White, the medicine show man. Two had come back quickly after they were sent out.

"No sir, we went into only one house, then Joey got scared and wouldn't go with me no more. I wasn't gonna do it alone." He passed over his shoulder bag. Inside was a fine set of sterling silverware, some silver goblets, a fat purse and a small leather bag filled with coins.

White glared at the offending boy, then backhanded him across the face, knocking him into the alley dirt. The ten-year-old wailed for a minute until he saw the gleaming knife at his throat.

"One more sound, laddie, and your throat gets slit!" White hit the boy again with a fist on the side of his head. Tears poured from the boy's eyes but he made no sound. "Lucky you're alive! You get no pay tonight, and you say one word to anyone about this, I'll track you down and slice your fingers off one by one and stuff them down your throat until you choke to death!"

Rusty White wiped beads of sweat off his forehead. He knew he was breathing hard, that his temper was raging again, but sometimes he couldn't stop it. He opened the leather bag, saw the gold coins and smiled. It might not be such a bad night after all.

Luke and his partner had worked all four of their houses and had found little cash, but did bring back two dueling pistols that should be worth something.

Rusty said they'd done good work, even though the take was small. He paid off the two boys and sent all three on their way. "We're through here," he told them. "You be good lads and keep your little mouths shut about this." He gave the two an extra dollar apiece and turned with Luke toward the wagon several blocks over.

"Do I get my two hundred?" Luke asked.

Rusty was furious in a flash. "You get what I give you!"

They walked another block. "A deal is a deal," Luke said. "You promised me two hundred."

"All right! Just be civil about it. Don't cause me trouble, Luke. I don't want to get angry with you."

Luke knew then that tonight had to be the

time. He had seen Rusty "get angry" at one of the boys in another town. Rusty had cut him into pieces with his knife. Luke had thrown up when he saw it and he knew he should have run away right then, but somehow he couldn't. Tonight he would. And his own knife would taste blood.

Inside the medicine wagon, they counted the money. Luke watched sharply. In the wallet there were one hundred twenty three dollars in greenbacks. In the leather pouch were twenty double gold eagles, four hundred dollars! Luke checked the bag again and found a large diamond ring. He set the value of the ring at a hundred dollars.

"I'll take ten of the double gold eagles," Luke said.

Rusty White glared at him for a moment, then shrugged and relaxed. "I'm not used to the new, more outspoken Luke yet," he said. "But as long as the rest of the bargain holds . . ."

"I said a deal was a deal."

"And I want to collect on it right now." Rusty caught Luke by the shoulders and pushed him to his knees, then pulled his face into the medicine man's throbbing crotch. "Right now, I want you to eat me. Then later on we'll use your other tender hole. Right now, you little whore!"

Luke knew this had to be the time. He had taken enough. He turned his head a little to get his breath, then his hand snaked into his pocket and he opened the snap-closed folding pocket knife with its four-inch blade. He always kept a razor-like edge on the steel blade.

He bent back suddenly and slashed upward with the knife, aiming for White's crotch. The blade missed, but bit a half inch into the medicine man's right leg, and he shrilled in pain, surprise and then fury.

Luke was in an impossible fighting position. Before he could jump to his feet, White kicked him in the chest, slamming him backward against the folding table. White fell on him, his one hundred and eighty pounds pinning the thin boy to the floor of the wagon. His hand slapped Luke's face from side to side a dozen times.

"What the hell you trying to do—castrate me, you little shit? You'll have to use a knife a lot better than that to hurt me." He had one knee on Luke's right bicep, crushing it, making the knife in his right hand useless. Luke tried to kick White but he could not touch him.

"Time you got a lesson, little whore. You're a male whore and a burglar and that's all you'll ever be. So don't get no more fancy ideas. You probably thought you were gonna kill me and take all my money and light out of town. Been tried a few times before, Luke. Didn't work them times neither. We gonna have a long, slow talk about that. Boy like you shouldn't never hurt a man who helps him, especially when you let him fuck your little ass."

White took a knife from his belt, sliding it from a hidden sheath. He brought the sharp five-inch blade across Luke's right palm. Luke dropped his knife and cried out in fear and pain.

"Don't hurt you much at all, Luke, not the way you gonna be hurting in a few minutes!"

Before Luke could scream again, White had pushed a handkerchief into the boy's mouth and tied another securely around his head to hold the gag in place. He ripped Luke's shirt open and drew three blood lines with his knife across the puny white chest.

"Such a shame, Luke. You were the best lover I've ever had, and that includes half a dozen women. You were the best!" He slapped Luke again, then caught both his hands and tied them together in front of him. White opened Luke's pants and slid them down, taking the short underwear with them.

Sparse, light colored pubic hair glistened in the lamp light over Luke's erection. The sudden fear had excited him, to his surprise and anger.

"No!" Luke shouted soundlessly, staring at his crotch.

"Oh, yes!" White roared. "You're just a little whore and you always will be!" White rubbed the swelling behind his fly, then shook his head.

"You like the knife, Luke? We'll see how well you like it." The blade flashed and a line sprang blood red down Luke's arm. It went deep and Luke screamed but no sound came out. His eyes were wide with terror.

Luke shook his head, eyes pleading.

Rusty White looked at the blood surging down Luke's arm. He rubbed his crotch again. Thoughts and emotions and yearnings slammed around in his head. Christ, but he was high! He was so excited he hardly knew what to do next. He slashed the outer arm now, and then quickly found a towel and covered up Luke's face where he lay on the floor.

Yes, better! Now there was no problem remembering the thing here as Luke. Forget the name, it wasn't important any more. Forget it!

The blade lowered again, slashed down one of the pure white, hairless legs, and blood gushed out. White stared at Luke's hard, twitching penis. Slowly he bent and kissed it, then took it in his mouth. A moment later he came away and shook his head.

Not this time, by God!

He cut Luke's other leg and watched the blood run.

Fantastic!

Exhilarating!

Tremendous!

He hadn't felt this way since that time nearly five years ago when he came west with his Uncle Zack on the wagon, and they found this little farm house that had a pretty mother and three daughters. Old Zack polished off the man of the house quick with his wet rawhide around the balls and the throat. Damn, what a day and a night that had been! They had taken turns and used up the women one at a time, then he personally had the fun of dispatching each one after the women slowly turned into raging lunatics.

He looked back at the thing on the floor.

Bastard! He had tried to kill Rusty White! There ws no doubt about it now, Rusty knew what had to be done. But there could be wonderment and marvels and joy even in difficult jobs.

"Boy, you picked the wrong man to run up against. You know that now. Shoulda been happy with that two hundred split. No, you got damn greedy! I warned you not to do that."

White opened his fly and pulled out his erection. He fisted it and pumped a few times, then grinned at the boy. White dropped to his knees beside him, grabbed the youth's still erect penis and cut a quarter inch slice from root to head.

Luke's screams came through the gag. He lunged upward, throwing off the towel. Fury and hatred seared through the air as Luke vented his agony, his frustration and his disbelief against Rusty White, then he passed out and fell back to the floor.

White hardly noticed. He knelt there, one hand busy at his crotch in his autoerotic flurry, and his other with the knife making small incision like cuts all over the unconscious form in front of him. None of the cuts alone would cause much harm, but they would bleed severely.

As his surging sexual heat increased, the knife dug deeper and deeper. White was panting now, his eyes glazed, his hands pumping rapidly. As the white hot surge came in his turgid phallus he moaned and the knife in his hand slashed at the untouched throat, again and again the knife descended until the whiteness of the neck bones showed through.

White gave one last moaning grunt of pleasure and fell backwards in the wagon, the knife dropping from his hand, a smile of total ecstasy on his face.

. . . .
. . . .
. . . .
. . . .

CHAPTER EIGHT

EARLY THAT SAME evening, the gathering at Mrs. Hillery Gregson's beautiful Spanish hacienda had begun promptly at nine. It was fashionably late, and she escorted Pastor Thompson from the revival to her courtyard.

The hacienda had belonged to a wealthy Spanish don during the early days of Santa Fe and had been built nearly two hundred years before. She had rebuilt part of it, added on to one wing with the same type of adobe construction, and regenerated the gardens in the courtyard that was fifty feet wide, and had an entrance and exit for buggies and riders.

"My, this is impressive," Pastor Thompson said, alighting from the buggy and helping Mrs. Gregson down. "Such a fine example of an old Spanish home. You must preserve it this way for posterity."

"I hope to do just that," Hillery said, pleased

at his comments. So many visitors thought the home quaint, but terribly out of date.

Three guests were already in the large living room, with its double fireplaces at each end, and furniture ranged around the other sides. A pair of musicians playing mandolin and guitar came strolling in with fast paced Mexican music.

She introduced the pastor to the early arrivals, and then to the others as they came.

Ten minutes later there were twelve people in the room. Half of them were dressed as if they had money. Interesting. But Erick Thompson was not at all interested in starting a church in Santa Fe. He was there only to make an impression on the lady. He had discovered that morning that she was indeed a widow. Her husband had been killed in a runaway carriage a year ago. He had been one of the wealthiest men in town, and now she controlled everything.

Erick's second purpose was to show his pleasure that she was heading the drive for a church. In the process he would be seeing her daily, and soon he would let slip his interest in her as a person and as a woman.

It might take a few days, a week at the most. This was the kind of lady you did not try to kiss after only a brief acquaintance. But he had the time.

The meeting was like those he had set up in other towns, and all for the same purpose, to select a target. An hour later it was over. They had elected Mrs. Gregson chairman. She would meet with the pastor the next morning, since there was no morning service, and they would lay out some additional plans. Then actual canvassing of prospective members would begin, an announcement in the paper would be made, and they would be on their way.

"Please come here for our meeting tomorrow, Pastor Thompson," she said at the door. The others had left, and Erick wanted to take the lady in his arms and kiss her a dozen times, then get his hands on her breasts . . .

"Pastor Thompson, I suggested meeting here tomorrow. Would that be all right?"

"Yes, of course. I was just thinking how lovely you look. I hope I'm not being too forward. My wife passed away a few years ago, in the big St. Louis flood. You may have heard of it." He turned away and brushed his eyes with his hand, then continued, "Well, I will certainly be here tomorrow. Did we set a time?"

"Ten o'clock, then we could have tea." She watched him closely. "Are you all right, Pastor? You look a little shaken."

"I'm fine. I just should not let myself get to thinking about Helen. I'm sorry. Yes, ten o'clock will be fine." He smiled at her, saw the hint of a smile in return and stepped into the cool summer night air. At the seven-thousand-foot level of the town, the nights were always pleasant, no matter how warm the summer days had been.

The fake pastor whistled as he walked the few blocks back to his wagon-church parked on the street. He had put his two horses in the livery stable for the night. He hummed softly to himself as he thought of the large amount of money he would get from Hillery Gregson, and how delicious she would be, naked and lying on her own bed.

He was sure there would be time. He had noticed the Medicine Wagon on the other side of town near the tenderloin district. That would be his brother Rusty. So he was in town and doing business as usual, Erick figured. That afternoon he had heard about a fight but it was all over by the time he got there. Two young hellions were about to shoot each other to pieces, but some stranger drew down on them and made them stop.

Erick had spotted the two gunmen; they were Birch and Piney, his nephews. That meant brother Zack was also in town somewhere. If he followed his usual pattern, Zack would lay low until both his brothers had time to finish their respective businesses. Sometimes Zack got itchy feet. If he did this time, one of the boys would make a late night call at one or both of the wagons and they would have a reunion in whatever house Zack had taken over. He was good at picking the places.

Lately the three men had been taking pains not to be seen together, to help avoid the lawmen who were looking for the Schmidke brothers. Erick laughed softly as he thought how many names he had used during the past two years. Schmidke had not been one of them.

He picked a new name for each town, which made it extremely hard for anyone chasing him. A man of the cloth had a lot of automatic defenses working for him, too. Everyone believed whatever he said. No one would suspect a preacher of anything bad, evil or illegal. And a pastor's title gave him immediate entrance to all the best homes in the city. It was the best diguise he had ever worked out to cover up his more profitable activities.

Pastor Thompson went up the steps and into his wagon. He never locked the door. Who would steal from a minister?

When Spur got back to the Santa Fe Carriage House and used the key in Annabelle's door, he remembered that she said she would have a surprise for him tonight. But there was little about the woman that he did not know intimately by now.

He closed the door and looked around the beautiful room. No one was there.

"Spur? In here."

It was Annabelle calling from the bedroom. That was a good place for a surprise. He tossed his hat on the love seat and went to the door. It was partway open. He walked in quickly, pushing the door aside.

On the bed was a scene that stopped him.

"I said I'd have a surprise for you," Annabelle said. She sat naked on her big bed holding a hand of cards. Across from her on the bed sat a dark-haired Mexican girl, also naked. The slightly brown-skinned girl had the biggest breasts Spur had ever seen.

"My God!" Spur said.

"I thought you would like Conchita. She works for me here at the hotel in various ways, and tonight she, and I, together, are all yours. Now don't tell me that you have ever enjoyed two beautiful women at the same time."

Spur stood there watching them.

Conchita turned toward him, got up on her knees and shook her big breasts, making them bounce and roll. She put her hands under them lifting them up so there was no sag. She laughed and looked at Annabelle.

"I think the big gringo is afraid of us poor little naked virgins," Conchita said.

Spur made a dive and landed on the bed between them, turned over on his back and pulled the girls on top of him, one with each arm.

"At a time like this, a man's got to be brave and face the music, even if he is petrified with fear."

"Honey, I don't care if you're petrified, as long as you're hard," Conchita said, and broke up laughing.

Spur reached up and nibbled on Conchita's breasts and she made soft little humming sounds. He looked at Annabelle.

"I don't understand. Don't you mind that Conchita is here? Aren't you jealous?"

"Jealous? Why? I figured out a long time ago that you're not going to stand still for a wedding ring, so why the hell not have a little fun while you're here? Conchita and I are best friends. Best friends share the good things they have. For a while I have you, so we share."

"What if I go for her big tits and kick you out of bed?"

"I'll punch you in the crotch and jump right back in. It's my bed!"

Both women broke up with laughter. Spur sat up and stared at the two naked women, the starkly white, slender Annabelle and the soft brown, heavier Conchita with the big boobs.

"Can you take care of both of us at once, Big Spur?" Conchita asked, smiling enticingly.

"I'll think of a way," Spur growled.

Conchita winked at Annabelle and rolled on top of Spur where he lay on his back. She pushed up and fed her big breasts one at a time into his mouth. As he sucked he felt hands at his crotch and knew it was Annabelle working up his head of steam.

The realization that he had two naked, sexy women working over him came slowly, and when it did he felt his blood begin to bubble and boil with desire. Conchita moved and her mouth covered his and the steam built higher. He could feel the heat of her body as she writhed and wiggled on top of him.

Then before he was entirely sure what was happening, Conchita moved lower over him, lifted his erection upward, and slowly backed her crotch down on it. He felt the slight resistance, then he plunged into her fully as she settled downward against him and growled deep in her throat.

Her black eyes sparkled as she looked down at him.

"Now we play cowboy, no?" she said and began to lift and lower herself, riding him like a calico pony. Each lunge brought a new surge of pleasure and desire to Spur.

When he looked up, he found Annabelle hovering over him. She kissed him and it was sweet, powerful.

"Now you're going to get your surprise," she said grinning strangely. She moved forward then, her body at right angles to his and gently lowered her crotch toward his face.

"Darling Spur, use your tongue inside me." She spread her legs and he saw swaying over him her pink love lips. They came lower and lower until he no longer could see them, only feel them on his cheek. He turned his head and darted his tongue out.

He heard her gasp in pleasure, and her voice was muted.

"Sweet Spur! Yes! I'm exploding. Please, yes, oh, God, yes!"

His tongue probed and probed, passing the nether lips, touching the soft bud of her clitoris, now risen and sensitive. He twanged it half a dozen times with his tongue and Annabelle began quivering and shaking in a climax. The vibrations rattled through her form and left her gasping for breath as she rolled away.

Spur looked down at Conchita, who had been

watching. She grinned and he saw sweat on her forehead. Conchita's breath came in gasps now; sweat dripped on him. He reached down and caught her swaying, bouncing breasts and she smiled at him, then he felt her surging in a powerful spasm.

"Oh, God! Oh, God! I'm going to die! I can't live through this. Sweet Jesus! So beautiful! I no can talk more . . ." Her eyes closed and her pretty face took on a look of ecstasy as her hips beat at his, countering his movements, pounding with steady hard thrusts.

Then she squealed and mumbled something in Spanish as her head began bobbing in rhythm to her hip thrusts. Spur felt his own floodgates open and now he joined in her thrusting, humping her into the air with each punching. She wailed, shouted in Spanish again, then screeched for fifteen seconds as she jolted and threshed and pounded at him again and again until her face was wet with sweat and she fell on him exhausted and unable to move.

Spur humped upward one more time and the whole world dissolved as he blasted his seed into the woman and then sucked in air through his mouth and nose and every pore of his body to replenish his oxygen-starved cells.

McCoy gave one final lunge and put his arms around the woman over him and closed his eyes. He could die happy now.

Five minutes later, Annabelle roused them and they sat up and took cold bottles of beer she offered. She nodded at Spur.

"Yeah, yeah, big city man. Of course we have

ice, and cold beer. You think we're out in the sticks? This is the capital of New Mexico, don't forget. Anyway, every hotel in town and about half the houses have their own ice house. We're at seven thousand feet, remember and we get all the ice we want in winter. We just cut it up into blocks with saws, and pack it in straw in an ice house that is dug halfway into the ground. We have ice all summer."

"Thanks for the guided tour." He reached over and petted one of Conchita's breasts. "How did you grow them so big?"

"I got up every morning and stretched them out, how you think?"

"I never grew any of my own," Spur said.

"I get from Mama. You should see *mi madre!*" She pushed his hand away. "Sometimes I wish I was tiny tits. Men all the time like big tits. Get all excited fast. I wear my clothes loose to hide them."

"Yeah, men are terrible. Sex crazy. Like two women who seduce one poor cowboy."

They hit him with pillows. The beer bottles fell to the floor and a wrestling match was in full swing on the bed. Conchita sat on Spur's head until he gently bit her bottom, then she jumped off and Spur rolled over and pinned Annabelle, who had fallen on her back.

In a heartbeat the wrestling was over and Spur bent and kissed Annabelle. "Thanks for the surprise," he said.

"You don't think it's over, do you? This is an all-night party. Conchita and I have a bet. I say five times, and she says you for sure can make love six times. So we have to test you out to see. Right now I'm going for number two. Do you think you can stand up under the testing?"

"It's a rough job to give a guy, but somebody's got to do it. But remember to be gentle with me."

She swung a pillow at him which he blocked then he kissed her gently, and Conchita sat on the side of the bed and cheered.

It turned out to be the longest, most exhausting night Spur McCoy could remember. But when the sun came up the next morning, he was still smiling.

CHAPTER NINE

ANNABELLE STARED AT Spur who sat on the edge of the bed in the morning light and put on his clothes. She was half asleep but shook her head in astonishment.

"*Eight times!* I still don't believe it. We must have lost track. I'm completely exhausted." She blinked and stared at him from drowsy eyes. "Where are you going?"

"It's morning. A man has to put in a good day's work, no matter what happened the night before." He bent and kissed her lips and lay her down on the big bed. She closed her eyes and had fallen alseep by the time he let go of her.

Conchita lay on her side, her big breasts billowing over one another toward the sheet. Spur reached in and petted the beauties and the girl smiled in her sleep and reached for him. He pulled back.

He had to get some kind of cover set up so he could go unnoticed on a door-to-door trip past the house where he suspected the rawhiders were hiding.

As Spur ate breakfast in the Carriage House dining room, a man tapped him on the shoulder.

"Mr. McCoy?"

Spur nodded.

"Sheriff wants to see you right away."

Spur stood, left the rest of his meal and followed the deputy toward the courthouse office of Sheriff James.

The sheriff looked worried.

"You must be right about them rawhiders being in town. All hell is breaking loose around here. We had five more reports of burglaries last night, with a lot of money, jewelry and silver stolen. Early last night there was a wild gunfight out in the north residential section of town and two horses were killed. The hardware was broken into last night and six long guns and all the ammunition for those stolen rifles was taken."

Spur scowled as the sheriff went on.

"Then this morning we found the body of a young boy. The poor kid had been tortured to death. Now how can you account for all of this?"

"Can't," Spur said. "Unless it *is* the raw-hiders. Could I see the boy?"

"Ain't pretty."

"I've seen corpses before."

"Hope not too many of them looked like this."

Five minutes later at the undertaker's Spur pulled back a sheet and winced. It was a torture murder. Looked like some he had seen by the Apaches when the Indians had lots of time, and a good hate built up against another Indian or a white. But there weren't any Indians on the warpath close around there, and none in town.

Spur looked away, then glanced back at the boy's face and turned his head so he had only a glimpse of the face. He did it twice more and then set his jaw.

"Anybody know who he is?" Spur asked.

"Don't think he's local. Nobody who's seen him so far knows him."

"I might," Spur said. "I saw him first night I was in town. He and another boy were slipping into the wagon the Medicine Show man is driving. It seemed like he belonged there by the way he moved."

"Doc White and his Medicine Show." The sheriff stroked his jaw. "Could be some connection."

"A lot of blood went somewhere, Sheriff. If we could find some in that wagon it would be a strong piece of evidence."

Sheriff James reached for his gunbelt, strapped it on and spoke quietly to one of his deputies. The man brought him a shotgun with a special short barrel. Sheriff James pushed two rounds of double ought buck into the tubes, and snapped the barrels shut.

"Let's go pay a visit to this snake-oil man," he said.

When they got there, the door canvas was open. There seemed to be no activity. Sheriff

James positioned deputies at forty-five degree angles to the near side of the rig so the men wouldn't shoot each other through the canvas. Then he and Spur walked up to the wagon and knocked on the wood bow.

There was no response. Spur saw that the flap was untied. He flicked one side of it up with his drawn .45. Then he lifted it fully.

No one was home.

The sheriff went through the opening with Spur right behind him. It looked much like other prairie schooners Spur had seen set up for travel and living. He smelled something, then he realized it was lye soap. Strong soap. He bent and looked at the wooden floor. It was made of one-inch boards glued together on the side, to make a four-inch thick floor, stronger than a framed floor.

Dark stains showed on the polished wood. Spur bent to sniff them but came up only with the smell of lye. A braided rug had been pushed to one side. The edge showed a dark stain. Spur sniffed.

Blood.

"Look at this," the sheriff said. He held a ripped-apart shirt and a pair of pants. "Looks about the size to fit that dead boy. Too small for a grown man."

Spur found a bucket pushed under the built-in bed. He opened the seal on top and squinted to be sure he saw right. The bucket was half filled with rags all stained a deep red. The lye smell was there but so was that of blood.

"Look at this, Sheriff," Spur said.

The sheriff touched the blood stains. Some of them were not dry yet. Red came away on his fingers. He smelled it.

"Let's find this medicine man," the sheriff said grimly. Outside, he sent his deputies fanning out through the town. They were concentrating on the cafes and restaurants that were open that time of day.

"I'll check the livery," Spur said. "Our Medicine man might have gone for his team with plans to move on."

"See that he doesn't move too far, but don't kill him if he draws down on you. I want him alive. I want him to hang high for this dastardly crime, if he's found guilty. We should be able to dig up someone else who saw the boy here. Let's move!"

Spur walked quickly toward the livery. He was only halfway there when he saw a man walking behind a team of harnessed horses driving them up the street. It was the Medicine Man, all right.

But he wasn't alone. The man had a stable boy with him, and a big .44 with hammer cocked was held by the boy's head as they walked along behind the team. Spur watched closely. There was no way he could shoot down the killer without the rawhider's gun going off, and it would kill the innocent boy.

Spur drew his .45 and waited behind a balcony support four-by-four as the team came up to him. He fired a shot into the air, then came down on the "doc."

"Give it up, Schmidke, this is the end of the line," Spur bellowed.

The man jumped in surprise, looked at Spur but kept the gun against the boy's head.

"Not true. This boy's life says it's not true. Put down your gun or I kill the boy."

"No you won't, Schmidke. Then your shield would be gone. You'll bluff it as long as you can, then kill the boy. I know how you think."

They kept walking, the team's harness jangling, trailing the pair of singletrees in the dirt street. Schmidke slapped the reins against the pair of blacks.

"You fire at me, the kid dies. Make up your mind."

"I'll check my bet. I want to see you hitch up the wagon and still keep the gun on the boy."

"Easy, you'll see."

Spur knew at once how he would do it. The boy worked in the stable. He could probably hitch up the big wagon better than the man could, and all the time the .44 would be against the lad's head.

Spur followed, watching the rawhider's second hand. He had given the reins to the boy now and walked directly beside him, the gun still in place. The rawhider would have a hide-out gun somewhere. Spur hoped he couldn't reach it without being obvious. If he got the hide-out there would be lots of gunplay.

Ahead, Spur saw the sheriff standing in the street. Spur ran to him and told him the situation.

"Hostage? The Bennett kid from the livery? Damn!"

"It'll take a miracle to save the boy," Spur said. "If we start shooting, Schmidke kills him. If we don't shoot, Schmidke gets away and will probably kill the boy as soon as he's free." Spur decided in a flash.

"Sheriff, let Schmidke hitch up and drive out of town. Follow him but don't attack. Keep a little pressure on him. I'm going to get a horse and keep up with him. Somewhere out there he's going to make a mistake. Have one of your men get me the best sighted-in rifle you've got, a long range one, one of the new Army Springfield rifles if you have one. Have your men stay with him until he gets out of town, then I'll take over."

"Should have a posse. Whole county is my jurisdiction."

"We don't want to spook him, just let him know he's still being followed so he won't kill the boy. I can handle it."

"From the way he's acting, there's no doubt in my mind that he killed the other boy."

"I'll bring him back alive if I can, but he's a rawhider. Keep other folks off the road so he can't get more hostages. Clear the streets if you can, now!"

Spur ran for the livery stable. He got the strongest, longest-lasting mount he could find, saddled him up and got back to the street just as the big wagon pulled out. A deputy tossed him a new army Springfield, the model with plenty of range. It came with a box of twenty five rounds. Spur wished he had more.

The boy sat in front, driving. Schmidke was inside somewhere out of sight, but, Spur was sure, with various peep holes so he could see what the sheriff was doing.

Two mounted men stormed into the street ahead of the wagon, turned and rode ahead of it, warning everyone on the street or driving a rig to get out of sight or to drive down a side street.

A half hour later the situation was exactly the same. The boy sat on the front seat driving the Medicine Wagon. The outskirts of Santa Fe were behind them as they began to wind toward the Jemez mountains.

Spur had held back, showing himself now and then so the rawhider knew he was there, but not long enough to offer a good target. He guessed Schmidke had rifles and pistols in the wagon.

A plan had formed in his mind before they left town, but he hesitated to use it. Now there seemed no other way. The boy's life was most important now. Spur would put down two good horses any day to save an innocent life. He found cover to his left and rode through pines and brush until he was a quarter of a mile ahead of the wagon, then worked back toward the trail, staying well concealed. He dismounted, took the Springfield long gun and found a log to sight over.

When the wagon came five minutes later, it was one hundred fifty yards from Spur's position. He lifted up, sighted in carefully and fired. The horse on the near side took the heavy .45 round in the head, and went down at once, front legs buckling, then rear legs as the momentum of the rig tangled the dying horse with the live one, which stumbled and pranced but slowed and stopped within five feet with her dead harness mate on the ground.

A scream of anger and fury came from the wagon. Then a dozen rounds blasted from the canvas top aimed in Spur's general direction. Schmidke jerked the boy off the front seat into the back of the wagon.

Spur watched. Now it was a waiting game. The rawhider would use what chips he had: the biggest was the boy's life. There would be no quick killing and then a shootout with the outlaw. He would hold the life of the boy as his best chance for escape. Spur had to make sure he kept thinking that way.

It would be a long time before anything happened, Spur was sure. The rawhider would try to figure out a way to escape. He would check all the possibilities first. The horse in the harness would be one chance, but a plow horse could not outrun the mount Spur had.

Spur tried to figure out what the man would do. Schmidke's answer came before Spur thought it would.

"You out there," the heavy voice came from the wagon. "It's the same standoff as before. I have the boy, and I'm leaving with him. You bother us, and he dies."

"Fine with me, Schmidke. The boy means nothing to me. You're in my jurisdiction now. Sheriff don't hold me down none. All I want is the posted reward on your dead carcass. Hell, I figured the kid would be dead by now and you'd want to shoot it out man to man. But I guess that's not your style."

Five more shots came toward Spur's location, but he had dropped behind the big pine log in time.

Now he lifted and put a rifle round through the top of the canvas well over either of the occupants' heads.

"Not much protection in there against hot lead, Schmidke. I might as well just use my dynamite and blow you both to hell."

"Bluff," Schmidke said and fired again. "You want the kid alive, otherwise you'd have drawn down on me a long time ago. So we compromise with the only real thing, what we're both more interested in than anything else . . . money. I put three thousand dollars in cash outside the tailgate, and the kid and I cut loose the dead horse and drive away. You get what you want—the reward money. Only you get it from me. And I get away to fight another day."

"Not a chance, Schmidke. I kill you, and I take your whole bank in there of over six thousand, and I get the reward money too." He put two rifle shots through the canvas, low and to the rear.

"Bastard! You killed the boy!" Schmidke shouted.

"Bluff, Schmidke! If I did you would never tell me—you think he's your shield. But he isn't. I figure I better just burn you out. Remember all that hoarded paper money of yours is going to burn too."

Spur had been working on a long shaft he had cut from a sapling. He fashioned it into an elementary spear. On the tip of it he bound dry grasses, and tied them on with tough wild vines. When he was through, he had a serviceable spear.

Quickly he made three more. One he left the grass off. That one was to establish the range.

Now he worked through the brush with the rifle and four spears getting as close as he could to the wagon. There was a chance that the desperado would cut a hole in the canvas on the far side, jump down and run to escape, but Spur didn't think he would. The fruits of a year or two of the rawhider's efforts were all in the wagon. He would leave it only when he was dead.

Spur checked his location. Now he was less than thirty yards from the wagon. He was sure he could throw the spear that far. He looked at the spears and changed the design. He sharpened the point, and tied the grass a foot in back of the tip. That would allow the point to pierce the canvas and hold the burning grass there long enough to set the heavy material on fire.

Spur used one of his stinker matches and lit the first bundle of grass, then lifted and threw the spear. It sailed well, nosed down but hit short. At least the fire kept burning all the way to the target. He tried again. This time the spear slanted to the side and missed.

The fourth spear he threw punctured the top of the canvas and clung there. The fire burned brightly for a moment, then seemed to slow. A moment later the canvas caught on fire and Spur put two more rifle shots through the top of the rig.

Over the sound of the flames Spur heard the call.

"Don't shoot! Don't shoot! We're coming out."

CHAPTER TEN

THE TOP OF the big covered wagon began burning fiercely where it sat in the middle of the trail out of Santa Fe.

"Did you hear me out there, goddamnit? I said to hold your fire, we're coming out."

"Come ahead, Schmidke, and bring the boy."

A small metal chest sailed out of the back of the wagon, then a wooden box, and a suitcase. Next the boy backed out, the pistol in Schmidke's hand again aimed at the youth's head.

Spur was in the same situation as before; if he shot the rawhider the boy would probably also die.

The two stood on the ground a dozen feet in back of the wagon.

"You want that horse to burn up, bounty hunter? Or can we go around front and cut her loose?"

"Cut her loose," Spur said. He ran from his

hiding spot into the open so he could follow the movements of the outlaw. There might be a chance he would take his eyes off the boy for a minute. All Spur needed was one free shot.

He had no chance. The boy cut the traces and then the connecting harness between the live horse and the dead one and slapped the back flank of the mare. She ran twenty feet down the road, then began grazing on the fringes of summer grass. The gun had never moved an inch from the youth's neck.

Spur checked the wagon horse. She would not be much of a saddle horse, but would work in a pinch. When he looked back, the place where the outlaw had been was empty. The boy lay in the grass where he had been pushed down, and the rawhider was gone. Spur now realized that cover grew considerably closer to the far side of the trail than it did on his side.

The boy was free—dead or alive, Spur didn't know. It was done, and now he had to think of the rawhider. What would he do? Where would he go? Spur lifted the rifle and shot the grazing wagon horse in the head. Even a draft horse like that one would provide transportation for the man. He winced as the mare screamed in her death throes.

At once Spur turned and ran for his own mount. The rawhider would try for it, then he could come back later for anything that was left in the wagon. Spur brushed past small trees and shrubs, darted through a ravine and saw his horse grazing where he had left her.

A shot smashed through the quiet mountain air and Spur dove behind a tree. Pistol. Ahead and to the left. Spur was closer to the horse than the rawhider. He fired twice into the brush where he figured the shot had originated and ran ahead to a big pine tree.

There was no response. He fired and ran again, coming to within fifteen feet of the horse. Another shot came from the brush to the left and Spur answered with three more rounds, emptying his six-gun. He was closer. Schmidke could not get to the mount. Spur had won the battle.

"Reckon as how you killed the other horse," the rawhider called.

Spur figured he was behind a big Ponderosa about twenty feet away.

"Right," Spur called back.

"Then that makes us even." Four shots came in rapid succession and the bay Spur was moving toward screamed a high shrill cry and went down. One last shot caught it in the head and it was still.

"I'll kill you before we're through with this, bounty hunter," Schmidke said, then all was silent.

Spur ran back toward the wagon, figuring the outlaw had gone in the opposite direction. Quickly Spur checked the boy. He had been pistol-whipped, with a bloody gash down his forehead, but he would live.

Spur hustled him into the brush and behind a big log.

"What's your name, son?"

"Terry Bennett."

"Can you find you way back to town?"

"Sure. I've lived around here all my life."

"You got most of the day, and it's only eight or nine o'clock. You stay here for half an hour or so, then start walking back. Tell the sheriff what happened. I'm going to get that rawhider."

The boy nodded. "He's a bad one. Pistol-whipped the night man at the livery, then grabbed me."

They looked at the wagon. The canvas had burned away, leaving the ribs of the top, but the fire had not caught anything else except one blanket that smoldered. Spur pulled it out of the wagon and let it burn itself out on the ground. He picked up the metal chest and the wooden box. Both were surprisingly heavy. Spur put them in the edge of the woods, covering them with leaves and some branches.

The boy watched him.

"What's in the boxes?"

"I don't know, Terry. But it was something that Schmidke must have wanted pretty badly. We'll save it so he can't find it. Now, you stay here for a half hour, then start for home."

Terry nodded and sat down under a tree.

Spur ran back into the woods where his horse lay and picked up the trail the outlaw made as he charged through the brush and woods. Every fifty feet, Spur stopped and listened. His guess was that the rawhider would run back to his brothers for help. There was plenty of firepower back in Santa Fe on his side.

The trail angled in that direction after two false starts. An hour later the trail came out on the track of a road. Spur sat down to rest a moment and think through his strategy. The easiest way and the quickest would be to stay on the road. Spur decided he could catch Schmidke faster that way as well.

He held the rifle at port arms and ran down the road at an Indian trot he had learned from a friendly Navajo. If he did it right, he could use up very little of his energy and move across the ground at twice the usual walking speed of about three miles an hour. A horse walks at four miles per hour. With his trot he should be able to cover six miles in an hour. He guessed they were not more than eight or nine miles out of town.

The first mile went well. He broke into a sweat and felt better, then he got into the rhythm of it and it came easier. After the second mile, he began watching for the other man's bootprints in the soft dirt. They were still there, and moving forward. Schmidke was not running—there was no digging in of the toe as a runner's footprint shows in soft dirt.

He would catch up with him during the next mile.

Spur came to a slight rise and slowed. Just over the rise he moved to the side of the trail and stood behind a ponderosa. Ahead he could see for two miles down a slight incline. There, four hundred yards ahead, he saw his quarry.

Schmidke sat by the side of the road under a tree. He had one boot off. Spur looked at the country. Sparse growth here, thinning out into a grassy valley that led down to the river. If he worked his way through the fringes of trees along the trail, he could make good time and stay out of sight. He did it.

When he got within two hundred yards, he would settle for one sure shot and rid the world once and for all of a Schmidke rawhider. Spur figured he had another fifty yards to go. He brushed past some brush and found only one opening ahead. Just as he stepped into it, he heard a swishing sound. He looked up in time to see a young pine tree slamming toward him. The pine had been bent back and held in place with some kind of trip device.

He fell to the ground and the sapling blasted past two feet over his head. It could easily have killed him, or broken both his legs.

Spur groaned and let out a feeble cry. If Schmidke was around close by, he would want to come in and finish off his victim.

For a moment, sounds came from directly ahead, but then they faded. Spur had crawled away from the trap site, and crouched behind a tree. It all had been a ruse, Schmidke showing himself in the trail with his boot off. And it had almost worked. Spur would be more respectful of his foe from now on.

More noise to the side, and Spur swung his .45 that way. The rifle was useless here in the brush—it took too long to lift and aim. The noise faded.

Spur looked around. There was a two-hundred-foot sharp cliff behind him. It rose upward steeply, and had a few trees on it. Ahead he could see the road and the mountain meadow that expanded into a wide valley through which the river flowed.

He should get back to the road. Schmidke must be well away from the area now.

The first sound was so slight he missed it. The next ones came so quickly he had little time to react. Then a boulder the size of a milk pail bounced past him. He looked toward the cliff. Dozens of boulders of all sizes were raining down, smashing forward over the downslope, tearing dirt and bushes with them. In a minute it would develop into a full scale landslide.

Spur leaped up and ran back the way he had come. There was a thick stand of three-foot ponderosa pines there. They might shield him, maybe divert the flow of rocks and dirt. A large rock bounced past Spur, then he charged the last twenty feet to the three big trees almost side by side and slid behind the largest.

Half a dozen times he felt the big tree vibrate as rocks and dirt and smaller trees slammed into the ponderosas. But all three held. The flow was reducing, it would be over soon.

Then a head-sized rock bounced high off one of the pines to his left, angling toward Spur. Only a lunge to his right saved him from being smashed by the rock. It hit the ground where he had been standing.

Far too late, Spur thought of the rife. The new army Springfield lay where it had been, but the rock had crushed it, broken the stock, bent the barrel at a weird angle and mangled the bolt and breech.

Now his weapons advantage was gone. No longer could he hope to stay well away and pick off the rawhider. The last boulders went rolling past, and he left his haven, running straight toward the trail. Many of the larger boulders were strewn over the roadway. He hit the trail and continued his Indian trot toward town. Wherever Schmidke was, Spur wanted to get ahead of him. He would plan his own ambush. It was time he went on the offensive.

After he had covered what he figured was two miles, Spur went to his side of the trail and began looking for a good spot to confront the outlaw. He wanted a narrow canyon, but there were none along here. He settled for a stretch with absolutely no cover. A house-sized rock near the trail was the only hiding place for half a mile each way.

This would be the spot. He sat down behind the rock to wait and rest a minute, reloaded his six-gun and looked at the remaining rounds in his belt. He had fifteen on each side. Not much of an ammo supply. If he were lucky, he would need only the five in his Colt .45.

Every two minutes, Spur edged to the side of the rock so he could see both ways down the trail. Schmidke would still be moving toward Santa Fe, where his reinforcements and resupply point was.

Spur's job was to stop him from getting there.

Spur had wished for some settlers, or farmers, or ranchers out this way, but he had seen no human habitation since crossing the river near Santa Fe that morning. It was afternoon now, maybe two o'clock. He set up a small sundial with three sticks and marked in the sand where the shadow of the long stick was. He would check to see how the shadow moved with the sun.

The small makeshift sundial had moved two finger-widths when Spur saw movement on the trail behind him. He watched closely and soon could make out Schmidke hobbling along using a cane. The trapper must have been trapped by his own avalanche, or one of his other booby traps.

Spur sat back and waited. In another five minutes he could tell if the rawhider still had his six-gun. There was a chance he had lost it. Should he take Schmidke in alive or dead? Usually the question never came up, there was no time to make a decision. In this case, there was time. Spur knew the sheriff wanted this man alive so he could stand trial.

On the other hand, how could Spur be sure that he could keep him prisoner all the way back to town? Many things could happen. Perhaps he should enact justice now while he had the chance. The more he considered it, the more he leaned toward gunsmoke justice this time.

He stared at the man coming down the road. He was a hundred yards off yet, and Spur could tell the man carried no gun. His holster flapped empty at his thigh, no gun was in his hand, and he doubted he would put it in his belt with a good holster. Spur smiled. He looked down the road the other way, as he had been doing regularly, and this time saw a trail of dust.

Someone was coming. A few minutes later he saw a buggy. The rawhider stopped where he was, still fifty yards from the rock. The rig came faster then. Someone stood up in it and let out a Rebel yell. The rawhider answered and did a little jig, bad leg and all.

"Where the hell you boys been?" Schmidke screeched.

The buggy rolled past the big rocks and Spur kept low and out of sight. Were these some more of the Schmidke clan? The buggy stopped and two young men jumped down. Spur looked in surprise at the men not more than twenty yards away. They were the same two he had stopped from shooting each other in the bar.

On the trail the three held a pow-wow. The older man the boys called Uncle Rusty insisted they go back to the site of the burned wagon to get what they could salvage. The boys insisted their pa had told them to grab him and get him right back to the house, if they could find him.

Rusty Schmidke kept arguing, but he was in no condition to win. The boys simply picked him up, put him in the buggy seat and turned the rig around. A moment later they sent up a trail of dust into the clear summer mountain air, as they hurried back toward Santa Fe.

When they were well clear, Spur stood and

stared after them, then holstered his gun. There was a time he might have tried to gun down all three of them, but he had no proof, damnit! The two young men might be clean as Sunday School teachers on a Sunday morning. Then on the other hand, they were Schmidkes. It was hard to believe that any of that clan could have clean hands.

Spur looked at the sun, checked back down the road and saw a figure coming toward him. It was the boy, Terry. He waited. They could walk back to Santa Fe together.

CHAPTER ELEVEN

"PASTOR" ERICK THOMPSON arrived at Hillery Gregson's hacienda promptly at ten that morning. He had spent an hour in the Third Street public baths, scrubbing his body within a shadow of its life, shaving carefully, and using a small bit of lotion on his hair. He had liberally slapped on bay rum and rose water after shave and put on his best black suit and cravat.

A small Mexican woman answered the door, and without saying a word showed him into a library.

"Señora Gregson be here soon," the woman said in heavily accented English, then vanished out the door.

He looked at the books. Few of them he recognized. His formal education had been brief and uninspired. He had used the Good Book to put a foundation under his preaching, and to obtain the needed polish and flair, but what his followers admired in his sermons was the total extent of his culture and education. His flock never knew it.

He could read well, but just never had the inclination. Now he took a book from a shelf, admiring the beautiful leather binding, and had just opened it when Hillery hurried in.

She wore a simple white dress that molded her upper body nicely. The dress had puffed sleeves and flared from the waist to the floor. He saw it was made of lace with an undergarment of some kind. For the first time he saw the swell of her breasts and he wondered if she had put on the dress to impress him. He hoped so. Maybe that whore was right about Hillery.

"Mrs. Gregson! Simply dazzling. That dress is so beautiful, and it sets off your hair and your eyes perfectly."

She showed a touch of blush at her long white neck, then her soft blue eyes gained control.

"Pastor Thompson, good morning. And thank you for your thoughtful words. I see now how you have been so successful in starting new churches. It's a gift." She smiled a moment. He took her hand and she led him to a patio where dozens of flowers bloomed and birds chirped and ate at feeders while two ruffled their feathers in a round bird bath.

"What a delightful spot!" he said. "I would love to have a place like this where I could meditate, and write my sermons. Somehow the outdoors seems the best place for me to compose."

"I like it here, too," Hillery said. "Many days I take my lunch here. Would you stay for lunch with me? I would be pleased."

"I would be honored!" He paused. "Now to work. How is your list of potential parishioners coming along?"

"Mrs. Darlow and I are working on it. As you can see, so far it's only from memory, but we have quite a group, about thirty families. One of us will be at each of your services, to ask people we don't have on the list about their interest."

"Yes, excellent, Mrs. Gregson."

"Pastor Thompson, I do wish you would call me Hillery."

He smiled, and bowed. "Mrs.—Hillery, nothing would give me more pleasure. And I ask that you call me Erick."

"I will. Erick, I will. Except when there are others around, when we should be more formal, don't you think?"

"I do."

The planning went on. They set another meeting for the next day. Lunch was a joy. They had tiny sandwiches, two kinds of tea and apple tarts for dessert.

Twice he saw her watching him when he was talking. He thought she seemed embarrassed, but he thought nothing about it when their lunch was over, he said it was time for him to leave.

"Oh, Erick, if you have nothing pressing, I would like to show you through the hacienda. I'm quite proud of the restoration."

126

He said he would be delighted. She led him through a dozen rooms, into the south wing, and then the west which was yet to be converted and restored. They were in a room that had once been a master bedroom. Only a bed was there now. The room was thirty feet long and twenty wide, more like a ballroom than a bedroom.

She started to go toward the door but tripped and fell against him. Erick's hands came out quickly and caught her and as he did, one hand brushed her breast and lingered until she found her balance. He started to move his hand, but her own came up and held his tightly on her bosom.

"Oh, my!" she said softly. "Oh, my!" She looked at him with the wide-eyed innocence of a virgin. Slowly he bent his face toward hers. Her eyes met his and for just a moment she hesitated. Then their lips met. The kiss was chaste and quick, but so important.

"Oh, my goodness!" she said softly. "That was so very sweet! I know that you are a man of the cloth, but you *were* married."

She moved her hand from his and eased it away from her breast.

"Hillery, I have been madly in love with you from the moment I saw you at the meeting. Did you know that?"

"Oh, my!"

"I knew you were a lady of quality, and that I would never in the world be worthy even to tell you of my devotion."

"Oh, Erick! Those are the sweetest words! When you told me about your wife, I wanted to take you in my arms and comfort you."

"It's not too late," he said softly.

"Oh, my!" She opened her arms and he put his around her, drawing her body firmly against his, crushing her breasts to him.

He kissed her again, and then again.

"My, I'm getting so dizzy—I should sit down."

"The bed," he said. She looked at him for a moment seriously, then he nodded. She smiled and he led her to the bed.

"The door . . ." she said. He walked to it and closed it and threw the bolt, then walked back to where she sat.

She patted the place beside her and he sat down, his arm around her. She lifted her face to be kissed again and then she sighed.

"Darling, sweet Erick. This is all so new, like a whirlwind. I had no idea you felt . . ." She kissed him again and he felt her lips part slightly.

"Erick, I want you to hold me and to kiss me, but we must go slowly. Today I want you to kiss me and touch me and to dream of how it might be . . . someday."

This time when he kissed her her lips parted. He darted his tongue between them and she sent her tongue in return. His hand moved down and caressed one of her breasts and she moaned in pleasure. He massaged first one, than the other gently, tenderly.

Before the kiss ended he had moved his hand

128

again, edging it past an open button and pushing aside her chemise. He touched her bare breast.

She shivered.

"Oh, darling Erick!" She shivered again, then kissed him with more force and desire than she had previously shown.

He started to lie down with her, but she resisted.

"No, no, Erick. Darling, I know what you want to do, but this is too sudden, too quick. I need time to sort things out." But she did not take his hand away. He unbuttoned the top of her dress and pushed it back, lifting the chemise. Her breasts were larger than he figured, pink tipped with upthrust nipples throbbing with excitement.

He bent and kissed one, and Hillery gasped, then quivered and wailed in delight as spasm after spasm of joy pulsed through her body. She caught his head and held it to her breast as she trembled in one climax after another.

At last she lifted his head and kissed his lips. There were tears in her eyes.

"Darling, it's been so long since I've even thought of making love with a man. And now— I'm so thrilled I can hardly talk!"

She hugged him, unmindful of her state of undress. He found her breasts with his hands again and petted them, then put his hand on her legs and began lifting her skirt.

"No!" she said sharply. Then she kissed him. "Tomorrow morning we'll have another meeting, here. I'll give you the rest of the guided tour and we'll end at my bedroom." She moved her hand over his crotch and rubbed the hardness. "Save this for me, until then!"

She stood, straightened her clothes and buttoned the dress.

"Now, Pastor Thompson, I have a lot of wonderful things to think about. Until tomorrow?"

He reached out and touched one breast through the fabric, then bent and kissed her.

"Until tomorrow. Oh, I would feel more secure if you give your servants the day off."

She lifted her brows. "I could get lunch for you myself! Yes, that would be fun. I'll see to it." She smiled radiantly, stood on tiptoe and kissed him again, then held his hand as they walked to the front door.

Their goodbyes held a special meaning. He turned and walked down the street.

Tomorrow morning. The clan reunion might have to be in a different location. He heard that Rusty left town in a hurry this morning with the sheriff chasing him. He'd found out what had happened. Tomorrow might be his last day in town as well, if it all worked out with the rich widow. He wondered how much cash and jewels she would have in the house. Erick grinned. He was damn well going to find out! Would it be too much to ask her for a twenty thousand dollar gift in cash to get the church donation drive started? he wondered.

He was moving quicker than he thought. The whore had certainly been right about Hillery. She had a hot little bottom and she wanted him. It would take her until tomorrow to convince herself that it was all right, and that they probably would get married.

Erick Thompson Schmidke laughed. What a surprise she was going to have tomorrow afternoon!

Zack White screamed at his two sons, Birch and Piney. They had been back with the buggy and Rusty only ten minutes and their pa was furious.

"You come back and left his wagon setting right there on the trail? How stupid are you guys? He said he's got three or four thousand dollars hidden around the wagon body!"

He whacked Piney on the shoulder. "Get those two wagon horses out in the barn and ride one, and get back out to that wagon. Hitch up the rig and drive it into the woods and then rub out the tracks so nobody can tell. You can do that 'fore it gets dark if you hurry. Take Birch along with you. Now scat!"

He went into the next room where Zelda was working on Rusty's right leg. The pants leg was slit to the crotch and she had the knee packed in steaming towels.

"Sprain," she said when Zack looked at her. She put her hand down the top of her dress and scratched one breast. "Stove up some, good as new in a week."

"Ain't got a week," Rusty said. "Got to get back to my wagon."

"Lucky you're alive, you fucked up bastard," Zack said. "Boys went out to hide the wagon. We'll go out tomorrow and get everything worth anything. You ride with us for a spell."

"You don't get to keep my goods, Zack. You tried that before."

"We're family, Rusty. Hell, I ever cheated you?"

"Damn right, every chance you get!"

"So don't give me no chances."

Rusty snorted. "Seen Erick? What's he up to?"

"Playing preacher still. Right now he's probably pussy-poking some rich widow lady. He told the boys he's got one on the string right now."

"About time," Rusty said. "Damnit, no, bitch!" Rusty said. He backhanded Zelda, spinning her away from the hot towels on his knee. "Look at that! It's swelling up more, not going down. I need some ice, you crazy bitch. Get me some ice!"

Zelda stuck her tongue out at him, turned around and farted, cracked a laugh and walked into the other room. "Fix your own damn knee, you weird little-boy lover! I got no time for bastards like you."

Zack laughed.

Rusty snorted. "Same old Zelda. Her pussy that good that you keep her around?"

"You should know, Rusty, you fucked her

enough."

"Hell, that was when she was young and pretty."

Zack nodded. "Christ, I should dump her, but she cooks good."

Rusty stared at his swollen knee. "Big Brother, bring me a bucket of cool water from the well. Could you do that for me? Got to have this knee fixed by morning so I can go out to my wagon."

Zack swore but went for the water.

An hour later the cold water started the swelling to go down.

"You had enough of city life, Zack?"

"Hell yes, no fun here. Too many people watching. Maybe tomorrow we'll pull out."

"First, Zack, you got to get me some new canvas for the wagon top from the hardware store, and then a team. I'm gonna fix up my rig again. Just burned off the top, I'd guess. Need some horses."

"Hell, we'll steal the horses. You pay for the canvas, I'll buy it. Goes against my grain, paying for stuff. What the hell, maybe just one more time." Zack stared at his brother.

"Rusty, same rules. You keep it in your pants around here. You start fucking around with Birch and I'll blow your head off. That boy's got troubles enough, you hear?"

"Yeah, I hear. Right now I just want to get this knee working again and get out of this town. Still don't know where that damned boulder came from. I was fifty feet away from the rock slide."

"Lucky it didn't hit you in the head. When in hell are them two boys getting back?"

CHAPTER TWELVE

SPUR AND TERRY Bennett were friends by the time
they had walked the rest of the way back to
Santa Fe. A rancher with a wagon stopped for
them about a mile out and they were glad for
the lift. Terry wanted to be a cowboy when he
grew up—that was why he was working in the
livery stable. Already he was a good rider.

Terry's parents were at the courthouse when
they arrived for a tearful reunion. They thanked
Spur a dozen times. The sheriff had told them it
would be a miracle of Terry survived his abduc-
tion.

After the Bennetts had left, Sheriff James
picked up a shotgun.

"It's time we go out there to the Galloway
place and find out who those people are and
what's going on. Bet you a lop-horned steer that
the Medicine Show man rushed right back to
that house, to his kin."

"We go in there now and we lose half your

deputies. You want to do that, Sheriff?" Spur asked. "We've got to wait until we have some real proof. Of course, it's your town."

"Hell, I don't want any of my men killed."

"Then let's wait a while. I'm out on my feet right now. In the morning I'll go out there on a delivery of some groceries. Reasonable that the emporium would send somebody to do that. I can get to the house and talk with somebody without any shooting. Worth a try."

Grudgingly the sheriff agreed.

Spur got up from the chair and groaned. "Never knew a body could be so tired in so many places. See you in the morning, Sheriff."

He limped a few paces, then got the kinks out of this tired legs and walked back to the Carriage House. The door of Annabelle's suite was unlocked. He walked in and slumped on the first chair he saw.

"Spur! What in the world happened to you?"

"Just a little tired. Two wenches kept me up all night last night."

"Wonder who the lucky girls were?" Annabelle teased. She wore a loose top and four petticoats but no skirt.

"You getting dressed or undressed?" Spur asked.

"Whichever you want," she said totally honest, no defense, no joking.

"Thanks. Make it dressed. I want a hot tub to soak my bones, a big dinner and ten hours of sleep."

"No fucking?"

He laughed. It bothered him when women used that word, but he nodded. "Yeah—no fucking tonight."

Conchita came in the hall door, saw Spur and waltzed up to him, pushing her breasts an inch from his mouth.

"Hey, *gringo*, you want to eat *mucho* titties?"

Spur chuckled and grabbed one, then let go. "Marvelous, but not tonight, I have a headache."

She laughed at him. "Still tired out from last night?"

"Right. I was the one who didn't get any sleep then or today."

Annabelle had Conchita arrange for the bath, and she went to the kitchen to bring up his dinner.

Both turned out to be hit performances. The women scrubbed Spur and he was so tired that their topless washing costumes never even caused his limp phallus to stir.

He had dinner of steak and four vegetables, chicken and heaps of mashed potatoes and gravy, coffee and thick slabs of rye bread and a big slice of chocolate cake.

Five minutes after the meal he crawled into bed. Spur never knew it, but that night a naked, interested, frustrated woman slept on each side of him.

"And so, my brethren and sisters in Christ, it is by His love that we are saved. It is nothing we do ourselves. It is by the grace of our savior

Jesus Christ, who died for our sins, that we have the opportunity to be saved . . . Yes, you're right, sister. There are a great many things that each of us must do to *keep* ourselves saved.

"Yes, there are the ten commandments, there is 'love thy neighbor,' there are dozens of codes of conduct that we must strive to follow, if we are to be true believers and children of God, who are saved in the Lord."

Erick looked down in the front row and found Hillery. He gave a small nod.

"And so we close our meeting tonight with the one abiding fact: Christians must live their faith, or it is a sham, a mockery, mere cant and a blasphemy unto the Lord!"

"Amen!" someone called.

They sang one of the old hymns that everyone knew.

"Brethren, there will be no offering tonight. You have been more than generous in the past." He held up his right hand.

"Shall we bow our heads for the benediction?" He recited a shorter one he had learned, and stood below the platform to shake hands with those who cared to.

Hillery was the last in line. When prying eyes had left, they went to the rear of the wagon in the shadows. He pecked a kiss on her lips and she melted against him. The touch of her body against his warmed his blood.

She shivered as she looked up.

"Darling, I want you so much it scares me! This morning was just . . . Well, I never dreamed that I could feel that way about any man, ever again. But you . . . It was simply wonderful! I can't wait for you to come tomorrow."

"I could stop by later tonight."

He left it hanging there.

"I'd love you to, but you can't. I . . . I just need a little more time to think about everything."

His lips brushed her cheek. "Tomorrow. I can hardly wait." He frowned slightly. "We must remember that we have a higher purpose too—the new church. We should launch the fund drive as soon as possible. I think now is the time."

She watched him. "Darling, I was going to save it as a surprise for you, but some stock paid a dividend this week and I want it to go to our church! It's ten thousand dollars. Should I give it to you now?"

He nodded. "The whole idea behind a drive like this is to get as much money as quickly as we can, so people say 'Oh, it's going so nicely, I want to be a part of it.' Then they jump on the bandwagon. If you could have it tomorrow it would get us off to a bangup start!"

"Yes! Yes, of course, I can have it tomorrow. It's in the bank. We'll have a ceremony the next day maybe, and get the drive started officially!"

He kissed her lips softly and she sighed.

"Hillery, I could never have dreamed of establishing a church here without you. Whatever would I have done?"

"Oh, Erick, you would have managed. It might have been harder, but you are so dedicated, so industrious. I love to watch you preach. You are so committed to your faith."

"Saving endangered souls is a serious business," he intoned sanctimoniously.

She hugged him again, then stepped back. "I must get to my rig. You be on time tomorrow, dear Erick."

"Hillery, I most certainly will."

"Goodnight." She turned and walked down the street twenty feet to where her driver was waiting. A moment later she was gone. He closed up the church wagon quickly, put away the lanterns and the portable pulpit, then set off walking quickly, following directions he had received that afternoon.

In fifteen minutes he was a mile across the spread-out town to a white clapboard house with two young pine trees in the front yard and two dormer windows. It had to be the right house. He went to the back door and knocked. It came open slowly but no one was there.

"It must be the Schmidke ghost," Erick joked.

A hoot went up from behind the door and Zelda jumped out where she could see him. She wore one of the clean dresses they had taken at the last house. It was too big for her, and bagged on her skinny frame.

"Erick, you sonofabitch, how are you?" Zelda screeched, ran and gave him a quick hug, then backed away as Zack came out of the living room into the kitchen.

He hadn't seen his youngest brother for almost three months.

"Hotter'n, Hell, if it ain't little buddy!"

"Howdy, Zack. Look like you're eatin' well."

"Tolerable." He grinned. "How's the soul-saving, church-raising game?"

"Tolerable. Might get even better tomorrow."

"Got a big fish on your line?"

"Seems to be. How did Rusty do? He get away?"

"No so the Hell you could notice," Rusty said hobbling into the room. He stared at Erick. "You still got those high and mighty ways?"

"Rusty, you want to catch a big fish, you got to know fish, you got to talk like fish, you got to think and act like fish. Same way you get the suckers to buy that snake oil of yours."

"Yeah, if it works."

"It's working. Least I ain't been run out of town. One of your cunt boys get out of line? The one at the undertaker's?"

"I don't talk about it."

"But you came running back here for help. You're putting us all out on a limb, Rusty."

"I asked him to come back," Zack said harshly. "I sent the boys out to help. And I still run what's left of this clan. You got objections, Erick, you draw a blade and we'll settle it." Zack stared at him.

Erick had forgotten how tough Zack could be. He wore a shirt with the buttons ripped off, his hairy chest and belly showing. He was sweating. His beard was matted, his face dirty and pimpled. A gash on his left cheek had not healed properly and oozed puss.

Erick shook his head. "I ain't challenging you,

Zack, but fact is fact. The sheriff finds him here, we're all in trouble. I got too much riding on this town right now."

"Then get your high faluttin' ass outa here," Rusty said, hobbling to a chair and easing into it. " 'Less you know how to make this god-damned leg better."

Zack got up and walked to the window and back. He looked at Rusty, then Erick.

"How much longer your little swindle gonna keep you here, Erick?"

"Fund drive to start a church takes a spell."

"How long? I don't aim to be here more'n a day or so. Too many folks asking questions about the old folks who used to live here."

Piney and Birch came into the room, bobbed their heads at their uncle and sat on the floor.

"You boys damn well better've hid that wagon good or I'll cane your butts till they bleed," Rusty said.

"We drove it into the woods a far spell, Uncle Rusty," Piney said.

"Nobody find it 'less they look real hard," Birch said.

"Nobody gonna find it 'fore we do. We'll drive out there 'bout noon tomorrow. This damn leg should be feeling better by then."

They looked at each other. Erick realized it had never been a closely knit family, not even when they ran two wagons together. Now they were further part than ever. In a way, he was relieved. He had managed to lift himself a little above the others.

"It could take me several days, even a week or

two, to get this fund raiser to a point where it's worth while," Erick said.

Zack scowled. "Hell, we got to move on, a day or two at the most. Get Rusty's wagon fixed up and he can come with us for a few weeks till he gets well."

"You sell here in town, Zack?" Erick asked.

"Hell no! Dumb ass! Can't you remember nothing I taught you? Get it on one side of town, and sell it in the next town a hundred miles down the road. Hell, you'll never learn. I'm going to bed. Got to get up early and get ready to move." He stood and looked at Erick. "Hell, little brother. You'll probably outdo all of us again. We'll be heading on toward Denver. You get there in August, we'll find you."

Erick waved at his two brothers, and went outside into the cool evening. He shook his head. The air seemed pure and clean out here. Had he been away from rawhiding that long?

As he walked back toward his wagon, he kept thinking about the next day. Ten o'clock. It would be a great day! By noon he could be ten thousand dollars richer! These days a man worked all year to make five hundred dollars as a clerk or laborer. Ten thousand dollars was what most men would earn in twenty years!

The thought bounced around in his head until he went to sleep.

CHAPTER THIRTEEN

A LITTLE BEFORE nine the next morning, Spur McCoy` had a cardboard box filled with groceries. He had made a stop at the general store and stocked up on some items he figured the Galloways might want: oatmeal, bacon, sugar, flour, and some tins of beans and peaches. Spur bought a billed cap and a pair of eye glasses with heavy black rims. He wanted a false beard, but had no idea where he could find one.

The poor disguise would have to do. He rode his horse, balancing the foot-square box on his leg. When he came in sight of the Galloway place he acted as natural as he could. He was coming on a visit to a friend.

Spur dismounted and left his horse tied to one of the trees in the yard and walked to the front door. The door looked like it didn't get much use. He knocked and waited. After a respectful time he knocked again. He heard movement inside and some whispers.

Soon the door edged open and he saw a thin-faced woman with dark, stringy hair. She looked out a three-inch crack in the door with a frown on her dirt smeared face.

"Hello. I was expecting Betty Galloway. Is she home?"

The woman opened the door more and he saw the dress was too fancy for her. It was much too large for her, too. "Course Betty's here. I'm her kin from Missouri."

"Betty told me to bring the grocery order over as usual. I come every week or so, knowing how they can't get around too good. Betty isn't sick, is she?"

"Nope. Nope, just resting this morning. Had a bad cough last night, wore the dear out. They both sleeping right now. I'll tell her you was here."

"Wanted to talk to her." Spur shrugged. "Guess I'll have to wait."

" 'Pears so."

Spur handed her the box of groceries. "Oh, she always pays me. Cost two dollars and ten cents this week."

"Two dollars!"

"Well, Betty said she wanted some sliced peaches."

"Just a minute." The woman vanished into the house and pushed the door closed but not latched. Spur heard more whispering, then the woman came back with two one-dollar gold pieces. Spur didn't like them, they were so small he often lost them.

"Much obliged. You tell Betty to get well quick." Spur turned and walked back to his horse. He knew there were two or three guns trained on his back. He hoped they believed him. If not, he was as dead as the Galloways must be.

But no weapon fired. He mounted up without looking at the house and rode away smartly toward town.

When he was out of sight, he gave a long sigh. The woman must be one of the rawhiders. She looked tough enough, and the dress obviously wasn't bought to fit her. Stolen. Spur knew it was down to the short hairs now. He was going to have to decide whether or not to go into that house the next time with his six-gun blazing.

The Galloways. If he could find their grave he would have all the proof he needed. That meant wait until evening. He hoped that everyone concerned would lay low today.

Inside the Galloway house, Zack watched Spur walk toward his horse. The double barreled shotgun was trained on him all the way. The other three men had guns on his back as well. When the horse hoofbeats faded, the men gathered in the kitchen where Zelda had been frying eggs.

"Cocksucker!" Rusty Schmidke roared. "I wanted to blast that sonofabitch right out of his socks! Told you he was about the size of the guy who bushwhacked me yesterday. Then when I heard the voice, I figured it had to be him. But by then he was moving out to the road and the neighbor couple came out their damn house."

Piney snorted. "That was the Jasper who stopped me and Birch from fighting down in that saloon. Hardnosed bastard. That was him!"

"You assholes are slow," Zack said snorting. "Shoulda figured it was him and invited him in for some lead breakfast. Now what the hell do we do? He must know we're here and who we are. He didn't buy that nap story about the oldsters."

"We bushwhack him!" Rusty said. "We send Piney to follow the fucker and see where he goes. Then we find out where he stays and we watch for him and gun him down."

Zack looked at Piney. "Yeah, go follow him. Now! Fast, damnit, before you lose him!" The younger of the two boys jumped up, grabbed his gunbelt and ran out the back door.

"Rusty, you can't go. Sheriff is watching for you, and too many in town know you. Me and the boys'll do it. Birch, go get us two rifles and twenty rounds for each one."

An hour later Zack and Birch lay on the roof of the Fancy Cat Saloon across from the Santa Fe Carriage House hotel. Piney had spotted the big rider going into the hotel. He was bound to come out sooner or later, and when he did he would be a perfect target for the old .56-50 Spencer that was Zack's favorite. He could pick the legs off a fly at a hundred yards with the weapon. He'd knocked over rabbits with the long gun at six hundred yards.

Birch was on the other end of the roof facing the street. It had a fancy grillwork they would shoot through and no one could see them. It was perfect. After the damn meddler was dead, they could go down a ladder on the back of the saloon and nobody would be able to tie them to the killing.

Piney was in the street, three doors down, leaning against the hardware store in a tilted back chair. He had his six-gun and he was good with it. Just in case this big man got away from the rifles, Piney could get him in the back as he ran into the street.

Zack grinned. No way this big hombre wasn't gonna be dead a minute after he came out the hotel door.

Spur looked over his gear in Annabelle's rooms. There was little he could do now until it got dark. His next best move was to ride back out to where that burned-out wagon was and see what Schmidke was trying to save in those boxes. He could take his time going through the wagon as well looking for more evidence. He'd take a deputy along with him to make it all legal and proper.

Spur cleaned his Colt .45 and then the Winchester repeating rifle, took out a supply of rounds for the pistol and an extra box of shells for the Winchester. He got his high crowned brown hat with the Mexican coins around the band and looked for Annabelle. She was in the hotel someplace.

He gave up looking for her and went toward

the front door. He had the rifle over his shoulder and the six-gun in his holster. The mount he had used that morning was still at the rail outside. He could get out to the wagon in about an hour, maybe a little more.

The stage pulled up in front of the hotel as he came out and a dozen people crowded around, greeting people and getting baggage down. Santa Fe had no railroad yet and the arrival of the stage was the biggest event of the day. He stepped around a pretty blonde lady who won a hug from her husband who got off the stage.

A rifle shot blasted into the morning air, and Spur felt something nick his thigh. He ran two steps and dove behind a six-foot-long horse trough and scanned the area. The shot had sounded as if it came from across the street. There were dozens of places over there a gunman could hide, between buildings, and on top of three of them. There had been only one shot. Most of the passengers and greeters huddled behind the stage.

"Get the sheriff!" somebody yelled.

"Shot came from the roof!" another man called.

"On top of the saloon! I saw the smoke," another voice called.

"Get somebody around there fast!" Spur yelled.

A pistol shot barked into the conversation as someone put a shot into the framework over the saloon.

Spur looked down the sidewalk along the businesses next to the hotel. He saw another man with a gun out, but he was not looking across the street. The young man was staring at Spur. In an instant Spur recognized the gunman, one of the two he had stopped from shooting it out in that saloon.

Spur's .45 was out—he had drawn it as he dove behind the water trough. Now he saw the young man run closer. He stopped at thirty feet and stepped behind a post holding up the second floor of the store that extended out over the sidewalk.

Spur stayed where he was, lying on his stomach, propped up on his elbows. The rifleman could still be sighting in on the area. He was trapped for the moment.

Before Spur could reason it out, the man ahead left his protection of the post and ran forward, straight at Spur, his six-gun bucking in his hand.

Spur felt the first slug whizz past him, then another hit the front of the trough. The Secret Agent fired twice. The first slug tore through Piney Schmidke's hand and dumped the gun from his grip. The second round caught him in the throat and tore a chunk out of his spinal cord as the big .45 lead missile ripped on through. Piney stumbled once, then dove off the boardwalk into the dust of the street. His eyes turned glassy as he stared up at the blue sky for a moment and screamed. Then his eyes shifted and stared directly at the sun, but he could see nothing.

"Look, that man is dead!" someone said on

the boardwalk. A woman leaned against the milinery shop, suddenly faint.

Someone shouted from the roof of the bar across the street.

"Hey, nobody up here, but I found an empty shell."

Spur was up now, caught his horse from the rail, mounted and rode hard for the alley across the street. He knew who he was looking for now. The kid was maybe twenty-two or three. Both had a strong family resemblance, he realized now. They must have been brothers. It had to be the same pair he had stopped from fighting.

The alley in back of the saloon produced nothing. They were on foot, but must have had horses close by. Spur rode a square around four blocks, looking for anyone riding hard. On the second block he saw two riders whipping their mounts north. He gave chase. For fifteen minutes they drove their mounts forward. Spur gained a little ground on them, but they were still almost a quarter of a mile ahead of him.

They came to a ravine and split up, going in opposite directions. Spur chose the smaller of the two men since it looked as if he had the slower horse.

But before he had gone twenty yards, the second horseman had stopped and began firing a rifle at Spur. The agent grabbed his own rifle, jumped off his horse and rolled behind some rocks.

Three more shots spanged off the rocks; then

there was only the silence of the New Mexico mountain air. Spur took a look and saw that the gunman had mounted up and ridden away toward a heavy patch of timber. He had gained five minutes' head start and at this distance, Spur knew he would never catch him in the brush. The first rider was out of sight heading back for town.

Spur gave up the chase and angled back to Santa Fe. He rode directly to the sheriff's office. The youth's body lay on top of a cheap wooden casket outside the door. A deputy asked everyone who passed if they knew the young man.

"No identification?" Spur asked the deputy.

"No sir. Nobody knows him. There was nothing on the body."

In the office the sheriff looked at him.

"You're bleeding."

Spur looked down at his thigh. "Just a scratch. That rifleman who was on the saloon roof. He missed. So did I. Chased two of them, but they got away."

"One didn't. Any idea who he is?"

"No. I broke up a fight between him and another kid I think might be his brother. They didn't like it. But don't seem like they would try to bushwhack me." Spur frowned and rubbed the back of his neck. "If that stage hadn't come in just when I left the hotel, that rifleman would have had me dead center. Stage shielded me most of the time. I was lucky."

"Maybe damn lucky." The sheriff handed him a wanted poster. It was newer than the other one they had found and was for a family of raw-hiders with the father called Zack. It said there were two sons aged twenty and twenty-two and a woman about forty.

"That corpse out there could be twenty to twenty-three. He could be one of the rawhiders."

Spur read the flyer again. Then he told the sheriff about his trip to the Galloway house that morning.

"Not possible, McCoy. That woman you saw couldn't have been a relative to the Galloways. The Galloways don't have no kin. They told me about six months ago. She was worried about what was going to happen to them if they got sick."

"The woman I talked to was about forty or so." Spur slapped his holster. "Sheriff, I'm going out there right now. I have to find some evidence we can work with. I think I can find a grave around the back yard somewhere. I want you to create some kind of a disturbance out front for them to watch. Arrest somebody, or stage a fake watch on a house, or something. And I want you to make up some special sticks of dynamite for me, with six inch fuses and caps. One way or the other, we're going to find out what happened to the Galloways!"

CHAPTER FOURTEEN

"Pastor" Erick Thompson Schmidke had left
Main Street ten minutes before the shootout
took place, and he was unaware of it. He was
blocks away ringing the bell at the hacienda
owned by Hillery Gregson.

She met him at the door. Today she wore a
low cut dress that showed a hint of cleavage.
Her hair had been brushed and combed a
hundred times, and her eyes misted with joy
when she saw him.

As soon as the door closed she ran into his
arms, pushing her breasts hard against his
chest, her lips reaching for his.

When the kiss ended she stared up at him,
still holding him close.

"Darling, where have you been? You're
thirty-seven seconds late! I didn't sleep a wink
all night thinking about you."

He kissed her again, hard, demanding. His
hand came away from her back and caught her

breasts and he kneaded them. He broke off the kiss, picked her up and smiled.

"Your servants are gone, right?"

She nodded.

"Where is your bedroom?"

"But first . . ."

"The only thing we're going to do first is tear each other's clothes off!"

She pointed the way, snuggling against him as he carried her, humming to herself, watching his face, then reaching up and kissing his cheek and his lips as he went up the stairs, through a hall and into her bedroom. It was almost as large as the one in the other wing. He lay her down on the bed and moved his mouth over her breast, sucking one into his mouth, and licking the fabric until he felt her shivering.

He leaned up and tore the thin fabric of her dress that went over her shoulder.

Hillery looked up in surprise, then wonder and desire flooded her face.

"Yes! Yes, tear it all off me. No one has ever torn my clothes off before!"

He ripped the bodice open and stripped off the chemise, revealing her breasts. He lifted her to a sitting position so he could play with her tits. She tugged at the buttons on his shirt, working her hand in to his naked chest.

Erick backed away and slid out of his shirt, then his shoes and stockings, and pulled his pants and underwear down together.

He stood over her where she sat on the bed.

Impulsively she caught his hard penis and stroked it. He pulled away and tore her dress down over her hips. Her petticoats went the same way and her silk drawers; then she writhed on the bed, nude and entranced.

Erick bathed her in kisses, starting at her forehead, then her eyes, and her ears, her lips, her chin and neck, then both her throbbing breasts. She shuddered in anticipation, shivering and moaning softly.

His mouth moved down across her stomach and her flat belly to the fringes of her pubic hair and she gasped.

"Oh, you don't have to!" she said.

But he continued, through the forest of soft brown hair until her legs spread apart in invitation and demand.

Erick licked the soft nether lips of her wet crotch and she jolted into a climax. Again and again she quivered, letting out a keening wail as her body vibrated.

"Oh, so beautiful! Darling, so wonderful. Oh! Oh! *Oh!* Darling, no one has ever touched me that way! Fabulous. Again, do it again! I can't move until you do it again!"

"Beg me," he said, lifting up. She kissed his lips, writhed against him, pushed him on his back on the big bed, and kissed his breasts, bit his nipples.

He caught her head and gently moved it lower.

"Sweetheart . . . ?" she asked.

"Beg me," he said again and brought her face to his erect, purple, pulsating penis.

"It's so beautiful!"

"Kiss it."

"Oh . . . Yes! Anything, darling. Anything you want me to do!"

She kissed his erection, held it tenderly, then experimentally let the purple-reddish head slip into her mouth. Erick watched.

"Yes, Hillery, beg me that way!"

She knelt there, her mouth working up and down on his swollen phallus. Erick moaned in pleasure, his hands reaching down and holding her breasts as she worked on him.

Once she stopped and looked at him.

Now his hips were grinding slowly, humping upward to meet her mouth. "Just a little more, Hillery. Just a little more."

She went back to work and he humped harder. She caught his rhythm. He groaned and then, with gentle hip thrusts, he shot burst after burst into her mouth. She gagged, then swallowed and stayed with him until he sighed and gasped for air.

She came away and wiped her mouth, then lay beside him on the bed. "I've never . . ." She began, but he kissed her and nodded, still breathing hard. As he recovered, she crawled off the bed and brought a small varnished jewel box about ten inches long with fancy copper hinges and fittings. She put it down between them on the bed and sat back cross-legged, watching him.

Erick looked at it, lifted up on one elbow and watched her.

"Pretty. What's inside?"

"Take a look." Her smile was filled with secrets and pleasure.

He undid the clasp and lifted the lid. Inside was more money than he had ever seen before. It was a stack of bills, with a hundred dollars on top, all tied with a pink ribbon and a small card. He opened the card.

"For my darling Erick and his favorite project." It was signed "Yours forever, Hillery."

He reached over and kissed her.

"I don't want you to be angry, and I know we talked about ten thousand, but I decided it would be better if I put in fifteen thousand. Is that all right?"

He set the box aside, touched the bills, then took Hillery in his arms and kissed her. He lay her down gently and lay on top of her and the kiss lasted and lasted. He could feel himself becoming excited again.

When their lips parted he watched her.

"Hillery, that is wonderful. You are amazing, beautiful, marvelous as a lover, and devoted. I don't know what to say."

"You don't have to say anything." She reached and caught his erection and guided it toward her moist crotch. "Just love me, Erick Thompson! I don't care what you are or who you are, or what you do or what you want to do, just make love to me all day and all night! And then all day and all night again, for years and years and years!"

It was past noon when they came apart for the third time. They nibbled on grapes and sipped brandy she had provided.

This morning Erick had actually been considering giving up his life of crime and settling down. What a woman to do it with! Not beautiful, but devoted and sexy, and most important of all, *rich!* He would never have to work again in his life. But would that mean he would have to follow through with starting a church and stay in his role as a preacher? That would be too much.

They made love twice more that afternoon and twice they talked about marriage. He brought it up first and she was surprised.

"Darling Erick! I'm thrilled and delighted that you are considering settling down. But you've been an itinerant for so long. Would you miss it? Would you be happy in one place?"

"Hillery, the wear and tear of constantly moving is starting to become tiresome. Frankly, I've been looking for some place to stay. Perhaps this is it."

She rolled on top of him, her breasts pressing against him as she hugged him.

"Sweet Erick! I don't care what you do or where you go, just so I can go with you! You don't even have to be a preacher. I have plenty of money for both of us to live on the rest of our lives. We could even move to Denver or New York City! A big city would be exciting. Yes! Let's talk about that."

They did for a while. Then she soberred. "I want you to know that I am serious. Come along." She caught his hand and took him down the hall to the library on the second floor.

There, behind a set of books, she showed him a safe. She turned the combination and pulled open the door. Inside was a cache of money. There were stacks of bills, even a small stack of Confederate money, and sacks filled with gold coins, all double eagles.

"This is some of the money I keep on hand. The bank has lots more drawing interest, and I have accounts in Denver and New York—stocks and bonds, even some railroad stocks that are going up in value every day. My late husband taught me about business. I'm making more money every day then I can possibly spend."

"You have a tremendous dowry," Mrs. Gregson.

"See that painting? It's quite valuable. It was painted by Rembrandt. It's worth thousands of dollars." She smiled, standing there naked. "As you can see, I am a woman of means. I just wanted you to know that if sometimes I seem to get too demanding, it's because I have been used to having my own way for so long."

He caught her hand. "Lets go back to your bedroom. I need to find exactly the right way to propose to you."

Her eyes widened and she caught her breath, pressing herself against him, hugging him tightly. They walked close together to the bedroom where they made love again.

About three that afternoon, they dressed and went to the kitchen where she made sandwiches and coffee for them. He insisted that she leave her blouse off so he could watch her bare breasts. She laughed and was self-conscious for a few minutes, but then after a while it seemed natural.

Erick had decided. He would marry this rich woman. They would go to Denver, he would "give up" the ministry and become a rich man for the rest of his life. No one could prove he was one of the rawhider Schmidke Brothers. He was in the clear. All he had to do was play it very carefully with his brothers for the next few hours.

They decided they would be married the next day by the judge in the courthouse. Then they would leave for Denver on their honeymoon, and find a house to buy there. Soon she would sell this place or they could keep it as a second house, and transfer all her accounts from here to Denver.

She watched him eat the sandwich of ham and slabs of fresh baked bread, and drink his coffee. "Darling Erick, I've never been more happy! I have missed making love this last year, but I never knew how much. I am enraptured—you have totally captured me!"

"You be careful or I'll rip that skirt off you and make love to you right here on the kitchen floor."

She giggled. "That would be fun, but I don't believe you can again so soon. Poor peter, I've worn him out. He needs a rest. And I'm going to be sore tomorrow. But what a glorious way to hurt!"

She kissed him and poured him more coffee.

"I'm delighted you suggested that the servants take the day off. It's been the most wonderful day of my life!"

"And mine!" He covered her hand with his. "We'll be married in the morning and get the afternoon stage for Denver. Then we'll begin our new life in the mile high city. Denver is getting to be quite a large town now."

She kissed his hand. "Darling, have I begged you enough yet?"

"What?"

"You asked me to beg you so you would do . . . do me with your tongue again."

Erick laughed. "My tongue still works." He stood and picked her up and sat her down on the edge of the kitchen table. Erick spread her legs and lifted her skirts around her waist, exposing the soft brown swatch of fur.

"Right here?" she asked. "On the *table?*"

"I always eat off a table."

He knelt in front of her and kissed around her pubic area, then used his fingers to arouse her, massaging her mound and her outer labia.

Then he moved forward, and nestled against her soft white flank with his cheek. His tongue darted out and she moaned. He touched her again and she wailed. When his tongue found her clit it was surging upward eager for combat and he twanged it from side to side with his tongue as Hillery wailed and climaxed again and again. She bent and grasped his shoulders and then held his head, forcing it harder against her crotch.

At last she sighed and lifted his head. She

kissed his wet lips and tasted some of her own juices.

"Now," she said with satisfaction. "*Now* I think that we're ready to get married."

CHAPTER FIFTEEN

Spur McCoy carried a cloth sack with him as he
pushed around a fence directly behind the
Galloway target house. He had his six-gun and a
short shovel. It had been five minutes since he
had left the sheriff. He and his men had worked
up a fake raid on a house about fifty yards down
from the Galloway place. They would be on the
little dirt street that went between the houses,
in full sight of those in the Galloway place.

It was supposed to keep the rawhiders inside
the house looking toward the front. It had to
work.

Spur crouched out of sight thirty yards from
the back of the Galloway barn.

Four pistol shots hammered into the Santa Fe
morning. It was still an hour from midday. Spur
listened and heard men shouting, then more
shots. After another two minutes he got the
barn between himself and the house and ran
forward across a pasture area, watching for

fresh earth. He had seen none as he waited. Now he scanned the ground closer for twenty yards on each side of him.

Nothing.

He got to the barn and looked around the outside of it. Two horses shied away from him. They were on long tethers so they could graze. The ground near them had been beaten bare of grass. Could be. Like burying someone in the middle of a trail drive route so the Indians couldn't desecrate the body. He pushed the shovel into sections of the barren, dusty section every three feet, but found it to be solid.

Inside the barn he looked in the stalls and straw covered areas, anywhere there was dirt underfoot. He was almost through checking the spots when he came to the last stall near the back. There had been a horse there, and the straw was matted down. He clawed it back with the shovel and pushed.

Soft!

He moved the spade and put his foot on it, it sank into the ground a foot deep. Carefully he began to dig. He had taken out only a dozen spadefuls of dirt when he hit something. He moved the shovel and lifted. A man's hand and arm came out of the dirt.

There would be two bodies in the shallow grave, he was sure.

He put the dirt back, spread the straw over the area, and walked to the front of the barn. Through a knothole he watched the rear of the house. Nobody moved. He heard more shots coming from down the road. The ruse was still working.

Spur ran out the back of the barn, taking the cloth sack with him. He left the short shovel and hurried to his horse. Before he mounted he opened the cloth sack and took out three of the sticks of dynamite. It was twenty percent, but all he could get. The blasting caps had been inserted into holes in the middle of the sticks, and six-inch fuses pushed in the hollow end of the metal cap.

The fuse had burned at a minute a foot when he tested it. He had about thirty seconds on each fuse. Too long. But sometimes the fuse burned faster. He took his knife and cut each of the eight fuses in half. Now he had eight small bombs that would burn for fifteen seconds before they exploded.

He mounted up and kept three of the sticks of dynamite in his left hand, and the stinker matches in his right. Spur rode up to the back of the barn using it as a shield, then readied the bombs and his matches and walked the horse toward the house. If the Schmidkes looked out the back, it would mean trouble.

A fresh burst of pistol and rifle fire came from the diversion down the road. Spur wanted to kick the bay and race her toward the house, but that could cause enough noise to attract attention. He gritted it out and a minute later he was near the back window. He had planned on using one stick in the kitchen, one in the side window and the third in the front bay window.

He struck the match and lit two fuses at once, immediately throwing one hard through the small kitchen window. Then he spurred the bay forward to the side window and threw the sputtering bomb in that opening. He charged forward to the front edge of the house, and started to light the third bomb just as the first one went off in the kitchen.

The blast belched smoke, fire and glass out the kitchen window. He heard screams from inside the house; then the second blast shattered the structure. He struck the match and lit the third bomb, raced around the corner and threw the dynamite through the bay window in front of the house and kicked the bay twice to keep her going flat out for the road fifty yards away.

The firing stopped down the road, and when Spur looked that way, he saw three of the sheriff's men.

The third blast behind him caused him to pull up the bay and wheel her around. The front half of the house had sagged. One man came running out, firing a pistol. An immediate response came from the lawmen who had been firing at the diversion house. The man Spur figured must be a Schmidke darted back into the smoking structure.

Flames licked out a window on the near side. The horses!

The back of the house was not covered. The rawhiders could go out the back, get the horses and ride away. Spur rode fast around the burning house and saw with relief that the horses were still staked out behind the barn.

Then where were the Schmidkes?

The sheriff and his men rode around the barn just then and Spur waved them over.

"Didn't see them out there, Sheriff. They might still be in the house or the barn."

The sheriff pointed at two of his men who rode to the house, dismounted and charged inside the burning building. They came out a minute later, one of them carrying someone. Spur rode up and saw the woman he had talked to at the front door the day before. The back of her head was blood red and pulpy.

"Dead," one of the deputies said. "Don't see how there could be nobody else in there alive."

The sheriff dismounted and all four of them stormed into the barn. It was empty of humans.

The lawmen came out of the barn and began looking around. In back of the barn about two hundred yards was a barn of the place across the field. As they looked that way, they heard a woman's scream followed by a pistol shot.

Spur jumped into his saddle and kicked the bay into a gallop. He put the barn across the field between himself and the other house. The rawhiders would go for the house to get weapons and maybe take hostages.

The agent leaped off his horse and sprinted the last five yards to the barn, worked his way around the near side and fell prone in the grass beside the front edge of the structure. He looked across thirty yards to the back door of the house. The screen door hung open, the spring broken. Smoke came from the kitchen chimney. A bucket hung on a rope over a well near the back door. Two golden cottonwoods spread across the front yard, towering over the house.

Spur heard noise behind him and turned as the sheriff bellied down into the grass beside him, a new army Springfield in his right hand.

"Got two men on the other edge of the barn to cover that side of the house," the sheriff said. "Seen anybody?"

Spur shook his head. "Woman screamed. Who lives here?"

"The Funkhowsers. They have five kids. He has a saddle shop in town. Best saddle maker in the state."

"So a woman and four kids inside."

"And some rawhiders."

"At least two, if we figure those Jaspers who bushwhacked me this morning are part of the bunch. Then the Medicine Man is somewhere. Call it three."

"Got to get them out," the sheriff said. He leveled the Springfield and put a .45 round through the kitchen window that faced the barn. For a moment there was no sound. Then a rifle barked from the house. The upstairs window shattered and the sheriff yelped.

"I'm hit!"

Spur had been moving as soon as the rifle fired. He pulled the sheriff back with him until they were out of line of fire of the upstairs window. The round had smashed the sheriff's shoulder.

"Sheriff. Sheriff!" a voice called from the

house. "There's no way you can touch us. You pull your men back and we won't kill any more of the kids. You understand?"

Spur looked at the sheriff; it was his decision.

"Tell the bastard he's bluffing. He has two minutes to come out or we'll dynamite the place into rubble."

Spur crawled up another six feet and shouted the response. Two more rifle shots ripped from the house. One missed Spur by an inch, and he moved back two more feet.

The back kitchen door swung open and something hurtled through it. The object was a child, three or four years old. The small form hit the dust and crumpled, not moving. Spur could see the child's head was a mass of crushed bones and blood.

The voice from the house came again.

"We don't bluff, Sheriff. Now pull back!"

Spur told the sheriff about the child.

"Christ! Animals!" The sheriff shook his head. "We can't risk the rest of the hostages. We pull back. Tell him."

Spur crawled forward and relayed the message. Two more shots slammed into the ground near his shoulder.

"Just target practicing," the voice from the house said. "I want all your men back to the other barn, two hundred yards over there. I'll have a rifle following you, so move it now. You don't move, we shoot the kids!"

Spur helped the sheriff to pull out. He told the lawman about the grave he had found in the barn. Both old people were probably in the same grave. The sheriff nodded grimly, the wound in his upper shoulder paining him. Spur got the man on his horse and had one of the deputies lead him back to the nearest doctor.

At the lean-to, Spur put one of the sticks of dynamite on the front wheel of the rawhider's prairie schooner and blew it off. The killers wouldn't be able to come back and get the rig.

He told the sheriff's men to fan out along the road, and make sure the rawhiders didn't work back into town. Spur then rode around the end of his picket line and studied the hostage house. They had weapons and horses. What would they do? He wasn't even sure how many of them there were.

As he thought about it the number came up three: Zack the leader of the clan, his brother the "Uncle Rusty" who must be the medicine man, and one of the younger boys.

Spur rode into the open about five hundred yards from the house and a rifle slug whistled past him. He jerked the mount around and got out of sight. Spur rode back to the barn. He sent one deputy out on each flank until they could see the front of the house. It was possible the rawhiders would try to leave that way. After that precaution, it was a wait and see situation. There were no more demands from the rawhiders.

An hour later they heard a scream and the woman was forced out the rear door. She was naked and had a rope around her neck. A booming voice cut through the silence.

"Sheriff, you've got five minutes to pull your

171

men back. If you don't we start shooting this bitch, first in the hands, then the elbows, then the feet and the knees. She'll be screaming to be killed long before she dies. Now get your men out of there!"

The senior deputy nodded at Spur.

"Sheriff would do it," the deputy said.

Spur agreed. "Pull everyone out. I'll stay in the barn. Make it a show so he thinks you're all gone. Best to form a rough square around the house, big enough so they can't see any of your men. My guess is they'll head out of town." The deputy nodded and moved his men away.

Spur sat by a knothole in the back of the barn watching the other barn two hundred yards away. He could see only two horses in the pasture behind the structure. They would need horses and supplies.

Then it was waiting time again.

An hour slid by, then another. It was mid-afternoon and nothing had happened. They were waiting for darkness. The woman had been pulled back inside. Spur heard a scream, then nothing more.

It was a long afternoon.

A half hour before dusk, Spur saw a young man race into the pasture and pull both horses into the barn. Shortly after that, three riders burst from the back door of the barn and rode away. All had sacks of provisions tied to saddles, and rifles in boots. Spur picked the largest man and fired four times with his rifle, but missed the moving, bouncing target. He jumped on his horse and went after him. The

172

man fired once over his shoulder, then concentrated on riding. He headed past two more houses, then towards the towering mountains toward the north of town.

Spur soon realized the man was an excellent horseman, and his mount was built for speed and stamina. It was going to be a long ride.

The trail left the scattering of houses at the edge of town and swung due north across fields of sparse grass and a few young pines, then turned west toward a long valley that angled upward and north into the mountains. The rawhider was a quarter of a mile ahead now, and Spur concentrated on keeping him at that distance as the two worked upward into the hills. There was no wagon road, no trail. They were cutting across virgin country.

Spur frowned at the gathering darkness. He would lose sight of his foe in another half hour, and then the outlaw would have all the advantages. He would keep moving, putting as much distance as he could between them. Spur would not be able to move, with no trail to follow. He would have to wait for daylight and then pick up the trail. The man was in his element. He would be twice as hard to capture out here as in town, and Spur McCoy was sure that he knew it.

CHAPTER SIXTEEN

SPUR MCCOY SAT on the horse and stared out into the darkness. He had reached the 8,000 foot level, a climb of about a thousand feet from Santa Fe, but still not at the end of the long gradual valley moving northward. The rawhider was somewhere in front of him. Spur had lost sight of him more than fifteen minutes ago when the man's sorrel vanished into a thick stand of ponderosa pine.

It was getting close to decision time. Surely the fugitive would keep running. He would not stop to camp and build a fire like some tenderfoot. A wild idea sparked in Spur's mind and he let it build and flesh out. Possible, yes, just possible. The rawhider was used to calling the shots, doing what he wanted to, taking over the problem and solving it his way. He might just try it.

Spur pulled into a thicket stand of young pines, and made camp. Quickly he built a small fire and let the smoke trail through the tall trees. Then he moved his horse two hundred yards into a deep thicket of brush where it should be well hidden. He went back to the fire, and made a dummy figure of blankets, with its head resting on the saddle. For a final touch, he put his hat over the place where the face of the man sleeping would be. As a final bit of bait, he lay his six-gun at the side of the blanket in quick reaching distance of the dummy. Spur built up the fire, using some heavy pieces of wood that would burn for two or three hours, then moved back from the site.

It took him ten minutes to find the spot he wanted. The position was a little higher than his fake camp, and gave him a field of fire of almost three quarters of the area in front of him. Anyone trying to sneak up on the camp would come from somewhere ahead of him. In the process, the attacker would become a perfect target.

That was the theory. Spur had decided that this rawhider would not keep on running. He would turn and fight, and he would do it the first chance he had when he would have the advantage. That meant darkness. He would hope that Spur would make a camp, and the best of all would be if his pursuer would build a fire. Spur would give him both.

He waited. Even from his position Spur could smell the smoke from his campfire. It drifted through the pine forest like a beacon, a foreign element that any woodsman would pick up in a minute. If the rawhider was coming back to find him, the fire would be a perfect lure, a highway of smell.

There was no way Spur could see the stars from where he lay beside a big pine tree and a flat rock. He guessed about two hours had passed when he picked up the first sign of company. An owl which had been giving out regular calls to the west of the fire suddenly went silent, then came winging through the trees on its nocturnal flight. Something had disturbed it.

Spur watched the area closely. For five minutes nothing moved. Then through the dusty gloom of the moonlight, Spur saw a shadow move suddenly from one tree to another.

Spur smiled. He was taking the bait! The rawhider was attacking the way a white man would, quick, sudden movements followed by periods of immobility. An Indian would use the opposite method. An open space that had to be crossed would be covered with infinite slowness. His shadow would merge with those around him and move so slowly that it would not attract attention to itself. The scout might look directly at the shadow of an Indian on the open spot and move on past it. Then inch by inch the Indian would be across the open area, and the unwary scout would have a knife in his back.

Again the shadow darted to the next cover.

There was no target, not yet. Spur lifted the rifle and held it ready. His fire had burned down to glowing coals, yet would give some light. Enough for a target was all he needed.

The secret agent admitted that the rawhider was taking his time, making sure. There had been no noise other than the usual night creatures—a night hawk, an owl or two, and far off, the screech of a mountain lion.

The shadow moved closer to the fire. Spur could see the glint of light off a blade. He lifted the Remington and zeroed in on the dark shape of the figure below.

In a sudden lunge, the form lifted the knife and thrust it into the blankets pretending to be a body.

Spur fired the Remington repeater. Four times he blasted shots into his target below. There was no cry of pain, no new motion.

Far off the echoing of the shots made their last feeble sounds and then were gone forever. Spur watched the area intently, but could see no movement.

Either he had killed the rawhider or missed him entirely. For another half hour Spur watched the spot intently, but saw nothing move. The rawhider could not be more patient than that. Spur moved away from his firing location silently, wormed into a bramble patch of thorny brush and nestled down for a nap. He had to have some sleep. The rawhider was either asleep or dead. He would find out in the morning. But if he didn't get some sleep now he would be in no condition to track anyone tomorrow.

Twice he awoke with brambles digging into his flesh. At least he was still alive. With the dawn, he was up and moving, silently, cautiously, toward his firing site. He saw his camp below, but no body. Using his best silent movement techniques, he circled the campsite twice, but could find no one lying in wait for him. That cleared up, he got his horse, rode to the camp and found where the blankets had been stabbed three or four times, and bullet holes in the nearby tree, but no body, and no blood.

Spur moved out on the trail, found the marks left by the horseman moving in the same general direction and followed them north into the mountains. He knew there was a stage coach road through to Denver, but the rawhider was not using it. A horse could move by a much more direct route then the stage, and quicker.

All morning he trailed the man he assumed was a Schmidke up the mountain through the thinning timber, until they came to an area where sheets of rock gave poor footing and a few signs of passage. But Spur was a good enough tracker to find the nicks and scratches on the rock to keep on the trail.

Now the route led up a narrow gully that would end in a high pass between tall peaks. There was only one way to go here. Spur kept watching the route ahead, always wary of an ambush. The trail narrowed again and up ahead passed between two giant boulders which had been loosened by the eternal erosion and freeze-thaw cycle perhaps hundreds of years ago and crashed down to the valley.

He moved cautiously around the first boulder and was just ready to kick the sorrel's flanks to urge her up the foot-high step when he saw a sunflash ahead off metal and dove off the side of his mount, hitting the rocks on his hands and rolling behind the boulder.

A second after his dive, the sound of the rifle shot came and the angry report of a lead bullet glancing off the rock and whining away into space. His mount had shied backward at the sound of the rifle. Spur grabbed his rifle from the boot and crawled ahead so he could see the spot where the rifleman had been. There was nothing there now.

Spur ran around the rock on the far side out of sight of the sniper's spot, and scurried a hundred feet along the trail where he was shielded from view ahead.

He paused at the last bit of cover, then brought up the rifle and charged the last twenty feet to the shelf of rock where the rifleman had fired.

There was no one there.

The trail took a slight down-slope here for a hundred feet and at the end of that Spur saw a horseman. Automatically Spur's rifle came up and he slammed four shots at the target.

Almost in slow motion the man in the saddle reared up. His voice screamed out an oath and he pivoted out of the leather and fell hard against the side of the canyon wall, then tumbled to the trail where he sat up holding his shoulder.

Spur put another rifle round into the dirt beside him, then ran forward.

"Don't try for the iron or you're dead for

certain," Spur called.

Zack Schmidke roared in pain and anger. Never before had he been in such a position. He darted his hand to the pistol on his hip, only to hear the rifle fire again. The lead slammed into his right wrist, breaking the bones, slamming it backward, leaving his .44 deep in his leather.

"Bastard!" he roared. He glared at Spur who walked forward, the Remington held at hip level aimed at the rawhider. Zack's left hand pawed at the Colt .44, got it half way out of leather before the rifle cracked again. The round bored into his left shoulder, jolting his arm and hand away from the gun, pitching him backward until he lay in the dust looking up at the mountain tops and the morning sun.

Spur stood over him, the Remington aimed at his forehead.

"Zack Schmidke?"

"Who the hell is that? My name is Phil Jones."

"That's as good a name as any other to hang by. You kill that child yesterday afternoon?"

"Wouldn't stop bawling. I told him to stop."

Spur had out his .45 Colt now and he shot Zack in the right knee. Zack screeched in agony, then in stark fear. At last his screams scaled down to sobbing and he looked up at Spur.

"Go ahead, kill me. I'm no good this way. Finish me off, damn you!"

"Not a chance. You're going to stand trial and hang. You want to walk back to town or ride your horse?" Before the outlaw could get out his reply Spur held up his hand. "Remember,

Zack, you've still got one more knee and two elbows I can shoot up. And right now I'd damn well enjoy the target practice on a cold-blooded killing machine like you!"

It was over six hours later that Spur came riding into Santa Fe with Zack tied to the saddle of the second horse. His wounds had been patched up the best Spur could do, using the rawhider's shirt for bandages.

Sheriff James met them at the edge of town, told Zack he was under arrest for seven murders, and that the trial would start the next day. The sheriff had his shoulder bandaged up but grinned through the pain.

"At least we got one of them. The other two got away." He shook his head. "They killed that whole family before they left. Just no way we could have stopped them. At least this one will pay."

Spur sighed. The bad ones just got worse. "This kind tend to stick together. The other two may be back to try to get this one out of jail. Better put on extra protection."

Sheriff James said he had already ordered it. "We found that old couple in the grave you told me about. We won't have much trouble getting a jury to convict this one. Wish we had the other two."

"Anybody checked through their gear in the wagon?" Spur asked.

The sheriff said nobody had. He sent a deputy with Spur and they rode out to the house where the wagon had been parked. First they used a pry bar and got a block under the front axle where the wheel had been blown off.

The inside of the wagon was a storehouse of merchandise, all of it stolen and all for sale. There was everything from silverware to fancy dueling pistols, envelopes of stocks and bonds and several metal boxes filled with gold coins and tied bundles of paper money.

"This whole thing should be taken down to the courthouse and put under official custody, so as much of it as possible can be returned," Spur said. The deputy went into town to bring out a wheelwright with a new front wheel. Spur kept examining. He found family Bibles, fancy sets of books, expensive china all packed in papers, and some paintings that looked as if they could be valuable.

Something kept bothering him. There were three Schmidke brothers. They had found two, and the two sons, evidently of Zack. Where was the third brother of the clan? Now that he had a start on cleaning out the rattlesnake nest of killers, he wanted to get them all. Maybe the third brother hadn't come to town yet. Or he might be here and they didn't know who he was. None of them were using their real names, which made it a lot harder.

The wheelright came and they worked together getting the new wheel in place and axle repaired, then hitched up a team and hauled the heavy wagon down to the courthouse where it was put under guard in one of the stables in back of the jail. The cash boxes, the paintings and the silver were taken inside, where the cash was counted, the silver inventoried and the stocks and bonds duly registered and put in the safe.

The sheriff looked at the names they had found and a few addresses.

"It's going to be next to impossible to find out who most of this belongs to," he said. "The cash will simply revert to the county treasury. Some of the registered stocks and bonds can be returned to estates or heirs. The negotiable ones are almost like cash."

He threw up his hands. "We'll have the county attorney take over the whole matter. The other goods will probably be sold at a sheriff's auction one of these days."

Spur realized he hadn't had a good meal in a day and a half, and no real sleep to speak of. He thought of the hotel, and a hot bath and a meal. Then he thought of something else.

"There's another wagon we haven't brought in, the one that the medicine man left town in. Tomorrow morning I think I'll ride out and see if I can find it. It could have something in it that might tell us who the third brother is."

Sheriff James waved him off. "Help yourself. One rawhider wagon at a time is enough for me to worry about."

Spur was more interested in the metal chest and the box that the medicine man had tossed out of the wagon. What was he trying to save from the fire?

First a fine hot bath, then some dinner, and then he would think about those boxes. Or would Annabelle have something to say about what they did next? Spur smiled, thinking about it. He had worked hard for two days. It was time he had some food and some relaxation. The government couldn't expect him to work all day and all night forever without some time off. Yes, that's what he needed, a little rest and relaxation.

CHAPTER SEVENTEEN

SPUR AWOKE THE following morning with Annabelle's head nestled against his shoulder and a sweet smile on her face. When he reached down and kissed her lips softly, she wrinkled her nose and giggled.

"Do it again," she said in her sleep and turned so her arm fell across his chest.

Spur carefully slid away from her and dressed. It was 5:30 and he had work to do.

At the sheriff's office he arranged for a deputy to drive two wagon horses out the road where the medicine wagon had been left. Spur would ride on ahead and find the wagon if it had been moved, and get it ready to be brought back to town.

He picked a new horse from the livery, a young black mare who seemed eager to get on the road. Her ears stood up and she kept pawing the dirt with her right front hoof.

Spur urged her gently on and got to the spot

in a little under two hours where the wagon had burned. He found charred remnants of canvas but no wagon. His first concern was the boxes he had hidden near the trail. He looked over the area, then walked to the spot and pulled the boxes from under the leaves and branches where he had concealed them.

The first was a metal box a foot wide and eighteen inches long. A hasp held a small padlock. Spur shot it off with one round from his .45 and lifted the lid. A two-inch deep tray in the top of the box held gold coins, packets of paper money, stocks and bond certificates. There was enough here to launch a good sized fortune. Under the tray were leather and felt pouches filled with jewelry, mostly unmounted precious gems: diamonds, rubies, and a few emeralds. Another fortune in the making. Jewelry that had been stolen locally could be returned, and maybe some of the cash.

But the rest was loot from probably hundreds of robberies around the country. The county coffers would get another bonanza.

The other box was wooden, the top secured with a strap with a buckle on it. Spur undid the binding and opened it. What else would the raw-hider value as highly as his cash and jewels?

The first item Spur saw was a family Bible, listing births and deaths in the Schmidke family for the past fifty years. Under it was a stack of newspaper clippings showing the early exploits of a gang called the Smith Boys. Later papers identified the gang as the Schmidke Brothers, and traced their degeneration from train robbers and bank robbers into rawhiders who killed for the sport of it.

There were wanted posters, warning letters, notices and one picture of one of the boys. The Medicine Man must have been the historian of the family. It all would be helpful in prosecution of the family members.

Spur put the two boxes back where they had been concealed, then began his search for the wagon. It was possible that the Schmidke's had sent someone back to hide it when they saw the man the boys called Uncle Rusty was so badly hurt.

It took him two hours to find the rig. At last his series of searching circles had come across the trail of the heavy rig as it had passed through a soft spot near a small stream. The wagon had been hidden in a tiny ravine, with bushes and branches cut from trees to conceal it even further. Spur checked it quickly and saw that only the canvas had burned off the wagon. The ribs were still in place and most of the contents had not be damaged.

Back at the trail he met the deputy with the wagon horses and led him to the rig.

It took them two hours to get the heavy wagon out of the ravine, through the soft areas and back to the trail. Spur lifted the two boxes into the back of the wagon from their hiding place and tied his horse to the back of the rig. He rode in the wagon sorting through some of the items on board. Most of it was day-to-day living items, but he was sure there would be more money hidden around the wagon once they began to search it in earnest.

He looked at the metal box. Money had never been terribly important to him. He had always had all he needed. His father was well on his way to being a multi-millionaire and it all would be Spur's someday. Still he wished he had more expense money to do his job, even to help some of the people who needed it.

He opened the case and sorted through the bills. Each stack seemed to contain a thousand dollars, the equivalent of three or four years' salary for a working man in that year of 1874. It was more than two years of his own annual pay.

One of the bundles had big bills in it and he saw it was marked with a slip of paper indicating that it contained ten thousand dollars. That would be a good expense fund for him. He slid the packet of bills into his inside shirt pocket behind his brown vest. He would find a better spot for it later. The county would be somewhat less rich, but they would never miss it, and Spur would be able to help a lot of people who needed assistance.

Spur got back on his horse and rode shotgun the rest of the trip back to town. There were still some of the rawhiders on the loose and he didn't want them hijacking this wagon.

Back at the court house he carried the two boxes in and put them on the sheriff's desk.

"Another small problem for you, Sheriff. Cash, jewelry, more stocks and bonds and a history of the Schmidke clan. Some of the

188

stolen jewelry reports might match some of the goods here. Anything new on the other two Schmidkes?"

"Not a whisper, but I'll bet they'll be showing up again. The kid and the other brother are both without funds or supplies. They'll need both before they strike out again. I've got my men watching for both of them."

"Anything on the third brother, the one we haven't seen yet?"

"Not a thing. We're watching." The sheriff looked at the cash in the box and shook his head. "A lot of good folks died giving up all this. I just wish there was some way we could get it back to their kin."

Spur went back to the Carriage House Hotel and slid the packets of greenbacks into his small leather case, just in back of the outer lining. It fit perfectly. Then he found Annabelle and took her to a late lunch in the dining room. But he was still worried about the other two rawhider brothers who were on the loose.

Rusty White was wishing he had some of his own magic elixir that he had sold to the suckers. Anything with alcohol in it right now would taste good. He lay on a grassy bank beside a tiny stream somewhere above Santa Fe. It had taken him most of the afternoon to lose the posse that had been chasing him.

By that time his leg had swollen so that he could hardly ride. He had spent the night in another small valley, moving for fear the posse would be back after him. Now it was clear they had lost him, and he could decide what to do. He had a rifle and pistol and a horse. Zack's planning had meant that they had each packed a pillowcase full of food before they left the house.

At least he wouldn't starve for a few days.

Revenge!

Zelda was dead!

Piney was dead!

From what he had seen on the trail, Rusty figured Zack had got himself caught by that wild man called Spur.

First things first. He had to get Zack out of jail before they hung him. Today, somehow he had to get Zack out of there. If he had two good legs he'd ride into town, shoot his way into the jail and give Zack a pair of six-guns, and they would blast their way out.

But he didn't, so he needed a plan. What? That new fangled dynamite they used on the house, the stuff that killed Zelda—he'd get some of it and blow a hole in the jail and get Zack out! Yeah! He had money. He'd hire some bum to buy the powder and fuse the caps. A guy had showed him how to use it one time. Yeah!

His leg had swollen again. But an hour or so in the cold water would make it feel numb enough to ride. He'd steal some different clothes, a hat and shirt off a clothes line somewhere and nobody would recognize him, especially not with his three day's growth of black beard.

Rusty's leg hurt worse than he figured it would when he tried to get on his horse, but he made it. Then he was farther from town than he had thought. It was almost supper time when he rode into Santa Fe and called a drifter over to him. He arranged for the man to buy six sticks of dynamite, two caps, and two foot of fuse.

The drifter looked at the two dollars with a glint in his eye.

"If you're not back here in five minutes, I'm gonna come dig you out of whatever bar you're in and shoot your balls off! You hear me, drifter?" Rusty snarled.

"Sure, sure. I warn't thinkin' about that. I'll get the dynamite. Hell. If I can earn a quarter that easy I'll sure as hell do it right!"

"Better, by damn!" Rusty said and waved him toward the hard goods store.

Rusty watched from the alley. The drifter came out with a package and walked straight to where Rusty still sat on his horse. He was halfway sure that once he got off, he wouldn't be able to mount up again.

Rusty checked the goods in the sack, the dynamite and the caps and fuse, then gave the drifter a quarter and an extra dime from the change.

"Now get out of here!" Rusty said, and wheeled his horse back into the alley.

He rode to the alley behind the courthouse and turned in. He had seen two deputies but they were not concerned with him on his horse. The jail was in the back part of the courthouse. It was on the ground floor, and there were bars on the windows. He lifted up in the saddle to look in the window, but his leg hurt him so much he dropped back down at once.

Tears of pain filled his eyes. The leg had to be looked at by a doctor. That would be next.

Quickly he pushed the detonating cap into one of the dynamite sticks, and fit the fuse into its hollow end. Then he wrapped the six sticks of powder together with the paper from the sack. Where to put it? There was a rear door. That would be the best spot. He rode up to the door. He could lean down in the saddle and drop the dynamite against the heavy wooden door.

The decision made, Rusty struck a sulphur match and lit the fuse. He bent low in the saddle and tossed the dynamite bundle a foot to the ground beside the door. Then he pulled the horse around and rode out of the alley toward the closest street.

He had left a foot of fuse on the bomb. That should burn for about a minute. The time seemed much longer. He turned his horse and moved partway back down the alley, sheltering against the wall of a building fifty feet from the jail.

A brilliant flash daylighted the alley ahead of him in the dusk of almost dark. The sound of the explosion shredded his eardrums as it roared down the alley. A hot gush of air slapped him in the face as it rushed by. Then he kicked the startled horse into motion and rode toward the jail. There was no wreckage in the alley; it had all blown into the jail. The door was gone. A section of the rear wall eight feet high and half that long lay in crumbled adobe rubble.

A deputy struggled over the pile of adobe. Blood streamed down his face, one arm hung useless at his side, and he was screaming for someone to help him.

Two more deputies rushed out, and helped the injured man to sit down next to the wall. A dozen men ran in from the alley. One of them was a doctor who attended the wounded deputy.

Now Rusty saw the sheriff stumbling through the wreckage.

"Dynamite—had to be a bomb back here by the door. Damn fool thing to do! Most of the damn door hit Pete. Killed him instantly. And there isn't much we can do for that rawhider. Zack's cell was just beyond the door and caught most of the blast. At least it saved the county a trial and the cost of hanging him."

The sheriff stood there by the wreckage as the men began to clear it away. He motioned to another deputy. "Get over to the hard goods store and see who bought dynamite the last few days. Not much sale on it yet around here."

The sheriff turned and stared at Rusty for a minute, then looked at the others in the alley who had come to watch the aftermath of the explosion. Rusty turned his horse and walked out the alley.

Zack was hurt by the blast? Zack was almost dead? It couldn't be. Not possible! He was trying to get Zack out of there, not hurt him! Rusty rode around to the street near one of the saloons where there was a boardwalk set up a foot above the dirt street. He slid off his mount, touching down on the boardwalk, favoring his leg. He tied his horse to the rail and stood on the boardwalk watching the courthouse.

People on the street buzzed with talk about the explosion.

A man in a black suit, black string tie and white shirt came by, talking to another man.

"Well, I just heard that rawhider is dead. The blast killed him sure as shooting. But the bad part is the deputy got killed, too. Wonder who tried to blow up the jail?"

Rusty felt tears rolling down his cheeks. Zack dead? That wasn't supposed to happen! He gritted his teeth, reached for his gun, and almost shot the man who'd told the lie. Then he held back. No, he had to get on his horse first. Then he would take out as many of these city folks as he could. *They* had killed Zack!

He stood on the boardwalk and looked at the saddle. It seemed higher than usual. With the help of the roof post he lifted his boot up and, working the horse around, finally got the foot of his good leg in the stirrup.

He was sweating, and still crying. Rusty felt a wave of nausea sweep over him. His leg burned like it was on fire. He'd have to get to a doc soon.

Rusty wiped the sweat off his face, then with both hands on the saddle horn, he lifted and kicked his bad leg over the mount. But his leg didn't make it. It hit the front side and slide halfway, then stuck on top.

The pain made Rusty groan. He bit his lip

until he tasted blood, then reached out with his left hand, lifted his pants leg and pushed the useless leg over the horse. He never did get that leg in the stirrup.

But he was in the saddle! He lifted his six-gun out of his holster and rode slowly down the street. A man came out of a saloon to his right, silhouetted in the light from the doorway.

Rusty shot him in the belly and watched him fall.

He kept moving slowly down the street.

Somebody screamed behind him. Rusty ignored it.

Another man came from a small cafe, and Rusty shot him in the chest at twenty feet. The man slammed backward and went down. Another man beside him drew his gun, but Rusty shot him twice before he could fire.

There was nothing frantic or fast-paced about Rusty. He rode slowly forward. The next man he shot came from the court house. He was a deputy and he returned fire. Rusty's shot had hit the deputy in the shoulder.

Now there was shouting up and down the street. The deputy fired twice more as Rusty reached for his rifle.

Spur McCoy ran out of the sheriff's office and saw the man fire his last pistol round at the deputy. Spur drew his Colt .45 and before the gunman on the horse could bring his rifle up, Spur put two heavy lead slugs into his chest, blasting him backwards off his horse, killing him before he hit the dirt of the street.

Spur ran up and stared down at the man in the fading light.

He recognized the man he had chased out of town.

"He's Rusty Schmidke," Spur said. "One more of the Schmidke brothers. He must have been the one who dynamited the jail."

The sheriff ran up, saw Rusty and nodded. "Four down, and two more to go."

CHAPTER EIGHTEEN

ERICK THOMPSON SCHMIDKE rolled over in the big bed and caught Hillery Gregson's breasts where they hung in front of him. She gazed at him and smiled as he fondled her.

Erick had never been able to resist a woman's breasts. There was something so pure and delightful and primal about them. The essence of a woman . . . and so enticingly beautiful.

They had put off the wedding a day. The judge was out of town hearing cases, but would be back tomorrow. Erick had moved his gear into the big bedroom. They told the servants that the marriage was set and there was a holiday atmosphere within the big house.

Erick had heard about the deadly shootout on the other side of town the day before from a deliveryman who brought ice to the house.

"From what I hear, the sheriff had some outlaws surrounded in a house, but the killers held some hostages and then got away. My brother-in-law is a deputy sheriff and he said it was a couple of wild killer rawhiders!"

Erick had discovered later downtown that indeed Zack and the rest of the clan had been chased out of town. He was betting they would all get away.

Then this afternoon he had found out that Zack had been captured and jailed. Erick sat and sipped a whiskey from a fancy goblet as he thought about it. Should he swoop down on the court house and try to rescue his brother? Or had he broken the family ties? Had he put all that behind him when he had asked Hillery to marry him?

Before he had satisfied himself with an answer, he heard the explosion downtown and knew it had to be either Zack or Rusty. He heard the news that both rawhiders were dead soon after it happened. Erick had finished his glass of whiskey, marched into the bedroom and made love to Hillery, realizing that he had made the decision before it had been made for him. All that family crime and killing were behind him.

Hillery traced his mouth with a finger.

"You look so sad, so worried. Darling, is anything bothering you?"

"All this killing! It grieves me that so many have died in this small town in the past two days. How can a loving God let this happen?"

She pulled his face to her breasts and stroked his hair.

"My soon-to-be husband, you must not worry yourself about that. You must learn to leave all that kind of religious worry to those who are active in the ministry. Since as of today you have retired as a minister, we have only to concern ourselves with our own interests."

She pulled his mouth to cover one breast and smiled when he kissed it.

"There, now, isn't that better?"

They both were still naked, lying on the big bed. He sat up and stared down at her womanly form. Handful-sized breasts, pinkly tipped; narrow shoulders, and a long neck. Her face was kind and soft, but not beautiful. Her waist had thickened over the years but her legs were still slender and graceful.

He stroked the softness of the fur at her crotch and then kissed her.

"Sweet Hillery, you are right. I must learn to concern myself with my new wife, and what is important to both of us."

"You will have certain responsibilities. You'll want to keep an eye on my business agents in Denver, to be sure that they are managing my . . . *our* affairs correctly. You'll be in charge, of course. Whatever you say will go."

"Well, it will take me some time to learn about everything . . ."

She smiled. "Not long. You are a smart man, you catch on quickly. You'll do fine."

Hillery stood and stretched. "Making love with you gives me tremendous appetite. Let's dress specially nicely tonight!"

He agreed and sat there still dazed, watching her begin to dress.

Slowly he realized that his life really was

changing. Zelda, Zack, Rusty and even Piney were dead. The only one who could tie Erick to the clan was Birch and the way things were going he couldn't last long. It was like a new birth for Erick.

He stood and went to the closet, put on his finest "preaching suit" and best shirt. It was going to be a night to remember, a night that would mark his final transformation from raw-hider and phoney preacher, to a man deserving of respect . . . and a damn *rich man* at that!

The same night, Spur McCoy looked at the flyer the sheriff handed him in the lawman's office.

"This came in today on the stage," the sheriff said. " 'Pears as how our third Schmidke brother has been right here in town all the time."

Spur glanced at the broadside. It had a line drawing of a man that looked somewhat like the other Schmidke brothers. He read the type.

"A man believed to be Erick Schmidke, one of the notorious Schmidke Brothers who are wanted for murder in six states, is believed to be posing as a itinerant preacher, moving out of Texas into the west with a 'church wagon.' He stops at towns, holds revival meetings, and at times pretends to settle down and start to raise money to start a new church. When sufficient funds have been raised, Schmidke vanishes out of town on a stage or train and is not seen again.

"Anyone with information concerning his whereabouts is advised to wire the nearest U.S.

Marshal or the following city police department-ments . . ." It then listed twenty southwest towns.

"Haven't had time to more than make a few inquiries so far," Sheriff James said. "From what I've found out, the preacher has left his wagon, given up the ministry and moved in with the widow Hillery Gregson, the richest lady in town. She's worth at least a million dollars, mostly in Denver banks."

"So the preacher made a good convert?"

"My sources say they tried to get married yesterday, but the judge was out on his circuit. He comes back tomorrow."

"Then it's time we pay the couple a call. With a rich widow on the string, he won't do anything stupid. He'll deny who he is, and we'll have a hard time proving it."

"The drawing will help," the sheriff said.

"But not enough. If he denies who he is, I don't think we'll have enough evidence to arrest him. And with the widow Gregson backing him, they'll be in Denver before we can get any evidence from one of those towns."

"So what can we do?"

"We smoke him out, get him so scared that he tries to cut and run."

The sheriff frowned. "Gonna take a lot of scare to get him to run away from a million dollars. This is the big strike he's been looking for."

"I know. That's why I'm going to visit the Gregson mansion tonight as Brother McCoy, a fellow preacher in Christ, for some spiritual sustenance."

"I hope it works. I'll have a dozen deputies outside the house covering every door."

A half hour later, Spur walked up the steps of the Gregson house and rang the bell. He had made a quick visit to the Carriage House and changed into a dark suit, white shirt and black tie. He left his six-guns in his room, and carried only a small Derringer in his boot as a hide-out gun. He had been digging back into his Presbyterian roots for some old-fashioned religion. He was going to need it.

The door opened and a Mexican girl smiled at him.

"Brother McCoy to see Mrs. Gregson," he said and stepped into the entranceway.

A striking woman of about forty came at once from the doorway. She was not plain, but not really pretty either. A kind of glow emanated from her. She was, Spur decided, handsome.

"Yes, I'm Mrs. Gregson."

"Praise the Lord! I was told that I could find you here and that you are a true believer and one who could help a newly dedicated servant of the Lord!"

She frowned. "I am a Christian, Brother McCoy, but I don't remember hearing about you in Santa Fe."

"True, I have recently arrived, and am looking for a base of operations so I can open a new church."

A man came through the door behind the widow. He was taller than she, well dressed in a brown suit, cream-colored shirt and flowered cravat.

"Mrs. Gregson is not feeling up to talking about her religious activities tonight," the man said.

He was Erick Schmidke, Spur knew at a glance. He matched the drawing on the poster.

"Pastor Thompson! This is a surprise, and a pleasure. I've been at some of your revivals. You are truly inspired by our Lord Jesus Christ! I am in awe of your way with words, how well you serve the Lord. It's an honor to meet you!" Spur enthused.

The rawhider showed surprise and anger for a moment, then covered it and held out his hand.

"Brother McCoy, it is good to meet you, but I'm afraid you've caught us at a rather bad time. You see, Mrs. Gregson and I are to be married tomorrow, and we will be going to Denver on our honeymoon. So as you can understand, we have a thousand small things to get done. If we could postpone our talk until we get back late next month, both of us would appreciate it."

McCoy shook his head. "No. Absolutely not! The Devil waits for no man! Do the Lord's work today! Thrift, obedience and labor in the vineyard of the Lord are my daily tasks! I can't shirk my duties as a Christian and a preacher of the gospel, Pastor Thompson. I respect your views, but I must ask for time to talk with you about my call to the ministry and a problem I've been having."

Schmidke frowned. He looked at Mrs. Gregson, then shrugged.

"All right. We can give you a half hour, but no more. There simply are too many details to take care of here before our important day."

"Brother, I understand. And may the joy of the Lord go with you in your new life of wedded bliss."

They led the way into a sitting room where all took seats in finely upholstered chairs.

"Now, first, let me assure you that I am absolutely certain of my vocation," Spur said intensely. "I have heard the clarion call and accepted it and am committed to preach the gospel of our loving Lord Jesus Christ for as long as I live."

Spur saw Schmidke move uncomfortably on the chair. Good.

"Pastor Thompson, would you tell me about *your* call to preach the gospel?"

"I really don't think we have time for that right now, Brother McCoy. Do you have any other questions I could help you with?"

"Yes, that problem I mentioned. It's a matter of the vow of chastity I have taken. In my last parish, a young lady was appealing to me. I longed for her. I lusted after her! How can ministers like us maintain our chastity and stay pure for the good of the church?"

Spur saw the widow turn her head and hide her face behind her hand. He figured she was laughing.

"Are you criticizing me, Brother McCoy?"

Schmidke's voice had taken on a sober, angry tone.

"Oh, because you are to be married? Not at all, not at all. I know most pastors are married. It just isn't for me. And I thought that perhaps you could give me some help . . ."

Spur stood and walked to the window. "Could we speak alone for a few minutes, Pastor Thompson?"

"Mrs. Gregson and I have no secrets from one another, we . . ." He paused. "Very well, come into the hall."

When the door was closed Spur's attitude changed.

"Hey, Thompson, or whatever your name is, I caught your act in one of them Texas towns. Figured I could string along and learn the trade. Got it down now, and all I need is a stake. I mean, if you're getting out of the business, I'd be willing to take your church wagon." He chuckled softly. "Looks like you've caught yourself a live one here."

"I really don't know what you're talking about! I . . ."

McCoy waved his hand at the other man. "Come off it, Thompson! I've been in three towns where you worked your church-starting racket. It's a beauty, and I want to do the same damn thing. You've been my teacher for the past two months!"

"I don't know what you're talking about," Schmidke grated.

"Don't admit it. I don't care! I just want your

wagon, if you're getting out of the business. You can do that much for me."

"Yes, take the wagon, and the horses, I won't be needing them. Now, will you leave?"

"I have to see your lady first. Thank her properly."

Spur went back into the room where Mrs. Gregson still sat. He took the folded wanted poster from his pocket and handed it to her. She glanced at it, then looked up, startled.

"Yes, I'm afraid it's true," said Spur. "We got word just today. As you can see, the resemblance is exact. There can be no mistake. We've been tracking this man down for three months now. Let me introduce you to the wanted killer whose real name is Erick Schmidke."

The rawhider turned as Spur said his name. For a moment hatred flared on his face; then his better judgment prevailed and he laughed.

"My name is Thompson, and I can prove it. I don't know what paper you have there, but it doesn't concern me."

The widow was frowning now. "Erick, all those scars on your body—where did you get them?"

"In the war."

"But so many?"

"The war, I told you."

"Then sometimes you talk in your sleep. You say some of the strangest things."

"Hillery, darling, you can't believe those lies this man is telling you. I am Erick Thompson, preacher of the gospel. I don't know who this man is, but he's obviously a fraud. I'll put him out of the house and we'll forget all about it."

"Erick, I wish it were that easy. Since we've met, I've been checking upon you and I can't find any trace of an Erick Thompson in St. Louis."

"You don't believe me?" For a second he almost exploded. Then Erick gathered his senses and suppressed his anger. "Hillery, I'll put this imposter out and then we'll talk about it."

"No, Erick. We'd better talk now. My lawyer in Denver wired me yesterday that he had no record of you or any Pastor Thompson. He suggested we postpone the wedding. I was going to ignore him. Come here and look at the drawing of you, Erick. It's quite a good likeness."

Erick walked to where she sat, took the wanted poster from her hands and stared at it. He read the words, looked again at the picture, then lifted Hillery from where she sat.

In a move so swift Spur had no chance to counter it, Erick pulled a Derringer from his inside pocket and held it to Hillery Gregson's head.

"You make one false move, *Brother* McCoy, and I blow this lady's brains all over the sitting room!"

CHAPTER NINETEEN

ERICK SCHMIDKE PUSHED Hillery toward the window and looked past the heavy drapes. He saw a man two houses down talking to someone in a buggy. In the opposite direction he saw another man examining the shoe of his horse's front hoof.

Spur McCoy nodded.

"You'll never find them all, Erick. But they're out there. This place is surrounded and there's no way for you to get out alive."

"The hell there isn't! A hostage is always worth at least a million dollars." He caught Hillery by the hair and pushed her toward the door, then looked back at Spur. "Don't make the mistake of thinking that I might not hurt the lady. She would have been worth a million to me alive and in Denver. Right now she's worth more than that; she's worth my life."

He twisted Hillery around so she protected his body.

"There isn't one chance in hell that you or the sheriff are going to shoot down the town's richest lady just so you can get to me. We'll meet again, McCoy, and I won't have to conserve my shots the next time. I want you cold, slab-dead!"

The pair vanished out the doorway and Spur moved cautiously to it so he could see them. He followed them toward the front door where he saw Erick pick up another weapon, a six-gun from the closet. Now Spur was more careful.

"You'll never get out of town," Spur called. He had drawn the Derringer but had no chance to use it.

"I'll get away, and take plenty of cash with me. This little lady will warm my bed and also be my ticket to freedom. You just watch me!"

Erick used the next five minutes productively. He kept the Derringer against Hillery's head as she opened the safe, took out all the cash and put it in a small carpetbag. He then moved her to the kitchen where he told one of the servants to saddle up two horses and bring them to the back door.

By this time the sheriff would know something had gone wrong, Spur hoped. He followed the pair but had no opportunity of stopping them.

Hillery had hardly changed expression during her ordeal. Spur decided she was frightened and angry, but holding up well. If they worked it right they might rescue her yet.

The argument came through clearly. Hillery was arguing about something. Spur edged toward a door in the hallway so he could see.

"I simply must have a divided skirt if I am to ride that horse," Hillery said. "It's been months since I've ridden, and in a skirt like this I'll only hold you up. It's just common sense to let me dress properly for the trip. You are usually more intelligent than this, Erick."

He scowled, motioned to her to move and she led the way to the stairway, the Derringer still pressed against her head.

Spur decided it was time to make his move. When they were out of sight, he ran for the kitchen, slipped out the door and caught the reins of the horses. He leaped aboard one, grabbed the lead of the other and rode fast down the alley and away from the house.

The sheriff rode up to meet him.

"He panicked, wants to run. But now he's lost his horses."

The sheriff nodded. "What will he do now, do you think?"

"Hostage demands. A carriage, I would guess. Might take another person from the house."

An hour later Spur's worst fears came true. Erick had come out of the house with the six-gun against Hillery's head, and two women servants tied to her. He demanded that a buggy for the four of them be harnessed up and brought around. They had a box of food and he had a rifle and three six-guns.

"Just stay back and don't try to follow us. If you follow us, I'll kill one of the women and dump her on the trail. Believe me, Sheriff, I'll do it. Now clear out! I don't want to see any of you by the time the buggy gets here."

They had all faded back out of sight. Sheriff James and Spur talked it over.

"He'll definitely kill both the girls if he thinks it will help him get away," Spur said.

"We can't have that."

"We'll let him go, let him think he's getting away clean," Spur said. "Only I'll be tracking him all the way. He'll never see me. When it gets dark, I'll move in and take him. The women won't be hurt."

"Be sure."

"I'll be sure or I won't do it the first night."

"I can't figure out anything better," the sheriff said. "Can I send a man or two along with you?"

"No, but you can send a man down to the store and get me a day's worth of traveling food. I can't remember if I had breakfast or not."

Erick and his buggy left about a half-hour later. There was no sign of the posse, but Erick knew the sheriff's men were around. He would have some surprises for them if they showed up. He had tied the Derringer against the side of Hillery's neck, and put a cord around the trigger. He would grab the cord and jerk it and the rich widow lady would die quickly. The two servants were tied together and roped in to the buggy. Both were scared to death and he knew would give him no trouble. If the sheriff or Spur McCoy followed him, he would kill one or the

211

other without a second thought.

Erick grinned as he cleared the last of the houses in town and headed along the trail north toward Denver. Once a Schmidke, always a Schmidke, he reckoned. It would be a long trip, but there were some stops along the way. He planned on holding the servants for not more than three days. By then he could tell if there was any pursuit, and he should also be able to eliminate McCoy or any deputies who were on his trail and be on his own at last. He hadn't decided yet what to do with Hillery.

Marriage would have been ideal, but that was impossible now. Too bad—he'd really been getting fond of her. He had about twenty thousand dollars from the safe and that would have to do. Yes, she would be eliminated when she was no longer of any use to him.

That problem solved, Erick laid the whip to the black pulling the buggy and moved up the road faster. He had seen no one following them yet, but he knew there was someone there, probably the man McCoy. He must be a U.S. Marshal, Erick figured.

Several hours later, Spur settled down three hundred yards from the hostages, watching. It was dusk and fast becoming dark. The tenor of the hostage situation had been established early on. Erick had stripped all three women to the waist, and forced them to stay that way. It was part of his plan to humiliate them and prove that he held their very lives in his hand. They must do whatever he said.

Spur figured the outlaw knew he was being

followed, knew someone was out there watching for a chance to blow him away with a rifle. Consequently, Schmidke had made every move with one of the three women clasped to his chest. There had not been a single chance to pick him off safely with a well-placed shot.

The sleeping arrangements were as Spur had suspected. Two women lay on one side of Erick and one on the other side, and a blanket covered them all. While Spur wondered what Erick was doing under the blankets, there was no chance he could draw a head on the man with the women so close to him.

That night when he figured everyone would be sleeping, Spur made his first move. He worked his way silently to the spot where the black had been picketed, studied the tie down rope for several minutes, then unwrapped a six-gun from the hookup, and let the hammer down softly. It had been rigged to fire if the rope was moved beyond a certain limit and had to be moved by a human hand to make it go off. After that, Spur led the black away into the trees, came out on the trail a half mile down and slapped the mare on the flank, sending her home to her stable in Santa Fe.

When daylight came, Spur heard Erick swearing before he saw him lift up between the three women.

Spur had been awake for an hour, and the new Springfield 1873 army rifle had been loaded and ready.

Now he moved his sighting slightly, refined his aim, and squeezed the trigger.

For a brief moment, it was as though time stood still.

The rifle cracked in the thin mountain air. Erick Schmidke sitting up between the still sleeping women had made a fatal mistake. He seemed to nod, then his whole body slammed forward from the force of the big .45 rifle slug that had bored into the back of his head, dissipating most of its force as it tore through his brain, pulverizing vital motor centers, and then exited through his forehead, tearing away a chunk of skull.

Two of the women screamed.

Another female voice spoke quietly, soothing, telling them that it was all right, that they were safe now.

"Mrs. Gregson," Spur called. "Are you all right down there?"

Hillery turned, and he saw that she was sitting up, still bare to the waist. She nodded.

"Yes, Mr. McCoy, we are all fine. Erick is dead, as you know." Her voice was remarkably self-possessed.

"I'm coming down," Spur said.

When he had moved the three hundred yards to the campsite, he found little change. The two servants sat numbly in the same spot. All three women were still topless. Spur noticed with interest the differences in the women's breasts. After all, he was something of a connoisseur. Mrs. Gregson's were pinkly nippled. The older Mexican girl's soft brown breasts were large with dark nipples and almost no noticeable aerolas. The younger Mexican servant girl's breasts were still forming with small nipples.

"Mr. McCoy, I hoped you were following us," Hillery Gregson said, standing to meet him and graciously holding out her hand as if they were at a formal reception. "I thank you for your heroic rescue."

He took her hand and smiled.

"Any time for a trio of beautiful ladies. But I won't demand that you continue to dress in this fashion."

The Mexican girls giggled and turned away. Hillery smiled.

"There is a certain innocent freedom this way, Mr. McCoy. But if the sight offends you . . ." She smiled again, making no move to cover herself.

"Not in the least! Perhaps we could talk about it at a later time," Spur said. "Now we should be getting ready to move back to town."

It took them all morning to make the trip. Spur's saddle mount was unhappy pulling the buggy, but at last Spur talked her into the task. The ladies had dressed once more and were chattering away as if nothing had happened by the time they met the sheriff's men who had followed them at a half day's distance.

News of the rescue spread around town quickly, and a crowd had gathered at the sheriff's office to gawk at the body of the third of the famous Schmidke brothers rawhide gang. Spur had then turned off with the buggy, taking the women back to the Gregson mansion.

As he handed her down from the buggy, Hillery Gregson held Spur's hand longer than was absolutely necessary. She looked up at him.

"Mr. McCoy, I would appreciate it if you could call on me this afternoon. I realize you're some sort of law officer, but I must insist on a reward for your work in saving my life, as well as that of my two servants. I'll expect you at three p.m. sharp." She turned and walked into her house with the air of a person who is used to being obeyed.

Spur tipped his hat and unhitched his mount, then rode back to the sheriff's office where they talked for a moment. Spur would send a wire to the home office reporting the demise of the last of the Schmidke brothers, and his work here would be done.

But there was still Mrs. Gregson. He had saved twenty thousand dollars that Schmidke had stolen from her, but somehow he had a feeling she would show him more personal appreciation than a reward of money.

It was almost three o'clock before Spur realized it. He was still in his trail clothes, but it was too late to change. When he knocked on the door at the Gregson mansion it opened at once and Hillery smiled up at him.

"Welcome, Mr. McCoy! I am delighted to see you. Won't you come inside?"

She was dressed in the shearest of silk fabrics, the material showing every voluptuous curve of her body as if the material wasn't there at all. It was slightly pinkish and lent an added touch of color to the scene.

He stepped inside and she smiled.

"I hope you like my new negligee. I've never worn it before this afternoon. Come into the sitting room for a glass of wine."

Spur nodded and dropped his brown hat on a settee. She led the way and Spur appreciated every sensual movement revealed by the negligee.

Inside the sitting room he saw the two Mexican serving girls. Now both were scrubbed until they shone, black hair pulled back and braided, and to Spur's surprise and delight, they both were naked to the waist, with only the wispiest of streamers of gauzy material draping from their waists, half covering the blackness of their pubic hair.

The girls served each of them wine, pouring it from a newly opened bottle into long stemmed crystal glasses.

Spur and Hillery Gregson sat on a small settee, just the right size for two.

"Mr. McCoy, this afternoon the girls and I are three women who owe our lives to you. We are now your slaves to do with as you wish, one, two or all of us. There is no greater gift one person can give another than the gift of pleasure. Any small thing we can do for you in return for saving our lives will be done with joy, excitement and total delight. What *is* your pleasure?"

The three women moved in front of Spur,

217

knelt and then bowed down before him.

Spur lifted his brows, then one by one lifted them to a standing position. He kissed each woman softly on the mouth, then kissed their breasts. He moved the two servant girls to one side.

"Ladies, I am honored by your gratitude, and your offer, but you have given me the pleasure of being able to continue your lives. That is reward enough for me." He motioned them out of the room.

As he did, Hillery caught his hand, pushed it firmly over one of her breasts and led him down the hall to her bedroom.

"That was sweet, what you told the girls. Both are still virgins. But don't think you're going to get off that easy with me!" In the bedroom she closed the door, pulled off part of the flimsy material so her breasts were bare and pressed herself tightly against him.

"Today you killed my fiance. I'm holding you responsible for taking his place this afternoon and all night. This was to be my wedding night. Can you fill the bill?"

"Hillery, I think I can fill any opening that one might have to offer."

She squealed in delight and fell backwards on the bed.

Spur shucked out of his trail clothes and tore off the wisps of silk still clinging to Hillery, then lay heavily on top of her. Hillery moaned in delight.

"Oh, yes! Before Erick, I had nearly forgotten what a good hard man's body felt like crushing me into the mattress! Marvelous!" Her hands worked between them, found his already erect phallus and massaged it.

"It's difficult for a widow to have any kind of normal sex life," she continued. "Most men respect you too much, and there is seldom a chance for a romantic involvement. So sometimes a widow has to take matters into her own hands." She giggled. "And I certainly like this matter that is in my hands right now!"

Spur bent and licked and then kissed and sucked on her breasts and brought a quick, hard climax racing through her. She shivered and moaned, then shut her eyes and wailed a dozen times before she relaxed under him.

"Glorious! And you aren't even inside me yet! This is going to be a beautiful and a *long* afternoon!"

Spur felt his own temperature rising. Ever since he had come into the house and been greeted by the frank display of female nudity, he had been growing more and more excited. Now he pushed her legs apart and settled between them. She murmured in encouragement. Then he reached down and lifted her legs, moving them high over her head and resting them on his shoulders.

"Like this?" she asked.

He nodded, probed, found her moist slot and drove inward, bringing a low scream of rapture from her. She adjusted her position and then began to move against him, looking up in surprise.

"I never knew I could bend this far!" she said

and giggled.

Spur leaned on his elbows and charged into her steaming center, feeling her gripping him inside with a regularity that drove him higher and higher and before he wanted to, he exploded with an eruption of white-hot lava that scalded them both. He let her legs down and fell against her in his own mini-death as they both gasped for air.

As they rested, the younger servant girl came into the room. She was naked now, and carried bowls of freshly frozen ice cream, made with a little hand-cranked ice cream freezer and ice from the ice house. The delicious confection had been sprinkled with chocolate drops and fresh cherries.

They ate the delicacy before it melted.

Hillery smiled at Spur.

"I hope you like it, that you like *me*. This doesn't have to be a one time celebration, Spur McCoy. I get to Denver often. We could meet there. I have enough contacts so we could enjoy ourselves in almost any manner you chose."

"I do have certain responsibilities."

"Your job? Pooh! You could resign and live with me. I have more money than both of us could ever spend."

"I enjoy my work. I want to continue doing it."

"But don't you enjoy this—me—just a little?"

"More than a little! This is the kind of life that can become intoxicating, addictive. But for a man there must be something more to life, something of substance, of value, some feeling of accomplishment and worth. Like today, I saved three lives. Every time I get nightmares about killing a man, I'll try to balance them against the satisfaction of saving a life or two."

"Men—I'll never understand them! Most men work all their lives so they can take it easy in their old age, so they will have enough money to relax and slow down. I'm offering you all that now, while you're young and vibrant and can enjoy it all, with me."

He lay on his back and she slid over him, dipping one breast after the other into his mouth for his willing ministrations.

"Do you like that?" she asked.

He nodded, not able to talk at the moment.

"Good. I'm going to show you other wonders which you'll enjoy even more."

She turned and found his limp sabre and began to revive it. Spur gave little cries of delight as her tongue entranced him and soon he was eager to invade her flesh once again.

Hillery got on her hands and knees and looked at Spur.

"Big Man, I have an opening you haven't tried yet. I think you should see if you can fill it as you promised."

Spur chuckled and found that he was up to the task as he mounted her again from the back and she yelped in sudden pleasure, then quickly cautioned him to be gentle.

This time they climaxed together and both wailed and roared with a total lack of inhibition. Afterward, they sprawled on the big bed in exhaustion and wonder and a new regard for each other.

A short time later she leaned over him and kissed her lips.

"Spur McCoy, I want you for my husband. Will you marry me, today?"

He watched her green flecked eyes, then slowly shook his head.

"Hey, the man is supposed to ask the woman. Are you trying to upset the whole set of mores, our code of social conduct?" he teased.

"Fine. Will you ask me to marry you?"

He watched her eyes, then leaned up and kissed her soft, quivering lips.

"No, because you would say yes, and I'm not ready to get married, not with the job I have. The whole western half of this nation is my responsibility. I travel all the time."

"Marry me and you won't have to work."

"We covered that."

"It's worth another try. My husband right before he died said he was worth four million dollars. There must be more than that by now. Are you turning down four million dollars, or me?"

He kissed her. "Both."

"Ingrate!"

"But remember I saved your life. You could be dead by now."

She stopped, wrinkled her brow, then kissed him. "Yes, I had almost forgotten. I owe you everything. So if you won't marry me, I can still offer you my body and my wealth on an anytime-you-come basis. Then I can give you gifts, and establish an endowment for you. Yes, there are many ways I can continue to thank you for saving my life."

She kissed him and rolled on top of him. "Promise me that you will give me the satisfaction of making love to you for twenty-four hours."

"Twenty-four. . . . Do we get to sleep any at all in between?"

"Sure."

"Done. We fuck for twenty-four hours!"

She blushed when he said the taboo word. He laughed and said it again, then made her say it out loud and they both laughed. It was going to be an interesting twenty-four hours.

CHAPTER TWENTY

THE YOUNG MAN in trail-stained clothes sat at the last table against the wall in the Silver Dollar saloon, one of the worst establishments on Santa Fe's main street. He nursed a beer and stared at the men around him through glazed eyes.

He had made his way back to town cautiously, and even now kept one hand near his six-gun, but there had been no hue and cry. No one was looking for a lone rider. There seemed no interest in him at all.

Not like the day they had chased him out of town when his mother had been killed.

The damn dynamite bomb!

He looked at his hands, flexed them, and then let them go limp. He would never strangle the man who had killed her as he had promised her. He stared at the men around him, drinking, gambling, grabbing at the round bottoms and breasts of the dance hall girls.

It wasn't fair!

Of course it wasn't fair, he had learned that years ago. It wasn't fair, but that was just the way it was.

Now his paw was dead. His Uncle Rusty had been shot down in the street, and less than an hour ago he had heard that his Uncle Erick had been killed while trying to get out of town.

Gone.

All of his family gone!

He wanted to lash out at someone.

He wanted to make love to someone.

It always happened. Every serious problem in his life, every crisis had always come down to this. To kill or to make love. He fingered his six-gun. He could kill four or five before someone put a bullet in his head. That would be the best way. Yes!

Then he thought of a soft body next to his, of his own sexual gratification rising to fever pitch.

He stood up quickly and went out the saloon door, his hands well away from his gun. The dry goods store. He was sure the small youth in the dry goods store had been watching him that day.

Birch walked directly to the store and opened the door. Two women were buying cloth. They finished their transaction and left. He was now the only customer in the store.

The clerk came from the far side and watched him.

"Can I help you?" the youth said. He wasn't more than sixteen.

Birch heard a catch in his voice. He stared at the boy's face. Then he knew.

"Yes, you can help me," Birch said. "And you know exactly how you can help me." Birch reached toward him but the boy backed up slowly, moving behind a screen that shielded the front of the store from the supply room.

They stood and watched each other. "What's your name?" Birch asked, his voice husky.

"Lester."

"Good. Lester, you know how you can help me, don't you?"

Lester nodded. He fell to his knees and leaned against Birch's waist, then his arms went around Birch and Lester kissed the fly of his pants.

"Oh, yes, Lester, I knew you understood!" Birch said. Quickly he opened the buttons of his pants and pulled out his erection. "Do it, Lester! Birch said softly, and the young man bent and took the phallus into his mouth. Birch erupted almost at once, holding Lester's head firmly against him. Then his hips began to move and he patted Lester gently on the back of the head.

"Again, Lester, once more."

The front door bell rang as a customer came in and Birch cursed. He helped Lester to get up.

"Get rid of them fast!" Birch commanded.

Lester went to help the man with some canvas, and when he came back several minutes later, Birch was furious.

"What took you so long? I said get rid of him, not wait on him. Did you lock the front door?"

"No—can't. Mr. Norton would kill me."

Birch fumed. "All right, take down your pants and turn around."

"We can't right here. It's too risky. Somebody might come in."

Birch thumbed back the hammer of his six-gun and put the muzzle against Lester's mouth. "Take them down and bend over, or you're dead."

Three minutes later Andrew Norton came silently in the back door with the change from his usual walk to the bank. He put down the bank bag on the counter and looked for his clerk. Lester was the best he had ever had work for him. Norton had made almost no noise coming in, and now he was curious, not seeing Lester immediately. Curious, he checked behind the front screen.

What he saw enraged him. Lester was bent over a straight-backed chair, his pants around his ankles, and some stranger was behind him snorting and wheezing and humping him in the ass!

Norton pulled from his pocket the pistol that he carried to the bank every day. He was a good shot. He fired just once. The bullet tore through the tall man's head and slammed his body to the floor on one side of Lester.

Lester jumped up and turned, stunned, protesting.

"Mr. Norton! I . . ."

"Lester, don't worry. He was raping you. I know how it can happen. Don't fret about a thing. Pull up your pants and get your clothes fixed. Then run and bring the sheriff. You tell him this man was trying to rob the store and I got back just in time."

When Lester ran out the front door, Norton put a wad of bills in the dead man's pocket and then waited for the sheriff.

He wasn't sure who he had killed, but whoever he was he deserved it. Lester was his! Nobody could love Lester but him! A few others in town understood that. This stranger didn't know, so he was dead. Too damn bad!

The sheriff arrived moments later. He looked at the man's face, and then nodded.

"Can't be sure, Mr. Norton, but I'd swear that was the third man we chased out of town a few days ago, one of the Schmidke rawhider bunch. You were lucky he didn't just kill both you and then take what he wanted. Tell me how it happened again."

Norton went through the story he'd concocted once more, feeling more than a little lucky that the rawhider had been looking for sex, rather than for money or supplies.

Sheriff James nodded. "Sure as hell matches up. He's a dead ringer for that other Schmidke boy who got himself killed. The county owes you a debt of thanks, Mr. Norton."

When the sheriff was gone and the last customer had left for the day, Lester and Mr. Norton went back to the cot in the small office as they did every Thursday.

"He made me do it, Mr. Norton," Lester whined, his face white with nervous fear.

"I know he did, Lester, don't worry about it. It will be another one of our little secrets."

"Yes, Mr. Norton," Lester said, and watched his employer lock the door. Then Lester began to undress just as he did every Thursday.

CHAPTER TWENTY-ONE

LATE THE FOLLOWING afternoon, Spur McCoy walked somewhat unsteadily down the boardwalk toward the Santa Fe Carriage House. He knew he had some luggage there, but his state of mind was not clear enough for him to be exactly sure just where it was or what his room number might be.

The quantity and quality of the wine at Mrs. Gregson's mansion had progressed during the evening, as one bottle after another was emptied. Most of the daylight and dark hours at the big house had blended into a fuzzy, sexy, wonderful blur.

Spur ran into the post holding up the overhand portion of the General Store, and one of the three old-timers loafing in a tipped-back chair leaning against the store front guffawed. Spur turned to glare at him, but never quite located the offender.

Once he reached the Carriage House he felt

more secure. He walked across the lobby, down the first floor hallway and turned in at the owner's room. He finally found the door, but there appeared to be bodies standing in front of it.

On closer inspection they turned out to be pretty ladies. On closer inspection, they merged into one pretty lady—Annabelle.

"Annabelle!" Spur said, surprised and pleased that he remembered her name. He reached for her but she batted his arms down.

"Can you tell me exactly where you have been for the past twenty-four hours, Mister McCoy?" Annabelle asked icily.

"Where? Certainly. Fighting desperados, criminals and rawhiders. I cracked the famous Schmidke brothers rawhider case. Ya know that?"

"Yes, I know that!"

She was mad but she was weakening.

"And I did it so I could come back and spend a week with you." Spur grinned. He knew it was a drunk, silly grin.

She frowned. "You're lying. You'll be heading for Denver and the train just as soon as the next stage comes through!"

"Honest . . . honestinjun."

"And you're stinking drunk!"

"No, not drunk. A gentleman . . . a gentleman does not get drunk on good wine. He gets a glow!"

"Drunk as a stinking skunk!" She sighed. "Oh, hell, come on in. I might as well sober you up and see what's left of you. That damn Widow

231

Gregson certainly has changed."

"Th . . . tha . . . thank you."

"Congratulations, you put two words together!"

Annabelle scowled at him, then led him to her couch, aimed him at it and pushed. Spur toppled on target and relaxed. He was snoring almost at once.

"Damn that rich bitch!" Annabelle said softly. She snorted and put a pillow under Spur's head. But she had him now, and she would keep him! But how would she work it? Spur had seen all the tricks. She had used a lot of them on him herself. By the time he woke up she would have some plan.

But four hours later she had nothing worked out. She sat with a cup of coffee and watched him sleep. He was restless, stirring. She guessed he would wake up in a few minutes.

When Spur came back to the conscious world half an hour later, his head was clear. He was rested and ready to do battle.

"That's not fair," Annabelle wailed. "You should at least have a massive hangover."

"Sorry," Spur said. "I never do. Too much clean living, I guess. Did I get any mail from the stage?"

"You weren't supposed to ask," Annabelle said. "Mail or telegrams always mean you have to leave."

"Not always."

She took three envelopes from under the doily on the end table.

"They came yesterday, but I couldn't find you."

Spur looked at two of the envelopes. They were from the Denver Chief of Police. Inside he found two wires. Both telegrams had been sent to the Chief, who was instructed to send them on the stage to Spur in Santa Fe. The wires had come from Washington, D.C. in a matter of seconds, then had taken three days to get from Denver to Santa Fe.

Spur opened the first one.

"Good work closing out Bank Robbery job. Are you sure about the White brothers? Last report on them was that they were in Georgia."

The second wire must have arrived the same day. It said:

"Schmidke brothers also known as White, reported in Texas, heading West. Make them your first priority. Report progress weekly."

Spur handed them both to Annabelle.

"See. These don't always mean I have to leave."

Spur read the next wire and frowned.

"Frank and Jesse James still giving local authorities trouble in Missouri, Kansas and Texas. Suggest a conference with you in St. Louis next month to offer Federal help to the states regarding these interstate outlaws."

Spur put that one deep in his pocket. It was the first time his superiors had mentioned any of the outlaw gangs that had developed from wild raiders such as Quantrill during the Civil War.

"What's that one about?" Annabelle asked.

"Nothing you can see. When's dinner? I'm starved!"

"The kitchen closed an hour ago! You expect me to keep it open just so you can eat whenever you want to?"

"Fine—I'll find something."

She flew at him, her hands like claws reaching for his face. He caught her and stopped the threat and held her firmly. Then the anger faded from her face and she reached up and kissed him.

"Spur McCoy, you make me furious, and then you make me turn to jelly. What am I going to do with you?"

"Put up with me as long as you can, then kick me out of your bed and tell me to get lost."

"Not in a million years, Spur McCoy. Not ever!" She unbuttoned the front of her dress, caught his hand and towed him toward the bedroom.

"I imagine the widow has worn you out, but I'm going to check and see. Then I'll let you rest up a little before we see if we can beat your eight-times-in-a-night record. Or was it seven? I've forgotten. Spur McCoy, while I have you captured in my bedroom, I'm going to love you like I've never loved you, because one of these days, you'll leave and you won't ever come back. That will be the time my heart breaks."

Spur picked her up and carried her into the bedroom.

The Schmidke brothers case was closed.

There would be another one all too quickly, perhaps even some work with local authorities on the Jesse James gang. But until then, he was going to take a few days to rest up and relax and eat and sleep and make love and pretend he was just an ordinary man.

Too soon, he would be back in the saddle as a Secret Service Agent.

Annabelle pushed one breast upward toward his mouth. Spur couldn't pass up the offer. He bent and kissed the warm, vibrant flesh and felt it pulsating with excitement and desire . . .